What No Child Should See

Donna DeLeo Bruno

Visit our website at www.StillwaterPress.com for more information.

First Stillwater River Publications Edition

ISBN-13: 978-1-946300-76-8
ISBN-10: 1-946300-76-4

1 2 3 4 5 6 7 8 9 10

Written by Donna DeLeo Bruno
Cover design by Kody Lavature

Published by Stillwater River Publications, Pawtucket, RI, USA.

DEDICATION

To Rosa Cotton

PART 1

THE INVADERS ARRIVE

CHAPTER 1

In 1941, the year I was 12 years old, the Germans entered my small town in the Provençal countryside. My older brother Jacques, 13, and I were living with our grand-mere in her large ochre limestone house at the top of the hill on Rue Savoir. Until the invaders arrived, it was a charming and serene place, a somewhat somnolent town along the river Rhone and surrounded by sumptuous fields of lavender waving lazily in the gentle breeze beneath puffy marshmallow clouds. Riotous color greeted you everywhere, especially in summer when scarlet red geraniums stood at attention in decorative black wrought-iron window boxes. In June the meadow grass grew high and prolific with delicately winged butterflies flitting over all. Most inhabitants of our picturesque village knew each other, many families tracing roots back generations. Jacques and I attended the local schoolhouse to which we walked two miles each day and over which our teacher Madame Hugot presided with order and routine. In addition to the visual beauty surrounding us were the blending aromas of freshly baked crusty baguettes, flaky and buttery croissants, and delectable fruit pies which wafted from the open doorway of the neighborhood patisserie we passed on our daily trek. Madame Rousseau, the owner, would call out "Bon jour!" to us from her shop with its cobalt glazed stone pots, lush and overflowing with delicate white daisies bobbing their heads, more scarlet gerani-ums, sun-yellow pansies, amidst long trailing emerald ivy. All was a whirl of dazzling color creating a sort of kaleidoscopic swash as we ran past. Once at our assigned places in school, we would stand and respectfully bow our heads to recite the Lord's prayer followed by the mingling of sweet youthful voices proudly singing the well-known French "Marseille." So, the day began in camaraderie and order. Yes, we too had the regular classroom bully, as well as the snobbish young lady who felt herself superior to all and carried herself as would Marie Antoinette of former times. But overall, a warm feeling was shared by most students, some like myself eager to learn new things about the world, to exercise our minds, to read fine literature, and at recess to share jokes and secrets with our favorite friends. My very best friend was Monique Char whose brother René, I think, favored me just a little. On our return home each day from school, he would lag shyly behind us on our upward hike to Grand-mere's, always hanging in the background, his eyes averted but ears attentive to our female banter. Only when we'd arrived at our destination did he barely lift his gaze and focus it entirely on me—his wide grin bathing his freckled face in sweetness as he timidly uttered,

"Adieu, mon amie, Jeanne Marie," laughing because he had created a rhyming couplet. My name seemed to roll mellifluously and deliciously off his tongue. I was just at that age when I'd become aware of such things, and it gave me a secret pleasure which, as yet, I did not entirely understand.

You might wonder about my parents. We had been living as a family in Lyon before my father Francois Molineau was conscripted by the Reich to work in a labor camp—*arbeitslager*—leaving my mother Cecille to support me and Jacques. When it became necessary for her to work, she sent both of us to Grand-mere in the countryside and each month sent funds for our maintenance. Although we did not see her often, we regularly received her letters inquiring about our well-being and accompanied by cash. With the arrival of the Germans, however, the regularity of her correspondence and every other sense of normalcy ceased.

CHAPTER 2

y brother and I had always been close, partly because of our nearness in age but also because he was my only sibling. Unlike other brothers I had observed, he welcomed me in his games and gave me equal choice in what we played. Although younger, I never felt his underling or inferior in any way. We rarely quarreled; and when we did, it was quickly resolved probably because we had no one but each other which my grandmother often reminded us. She always stressed family ties, possibly because she had no one left except my father Francois whose safety she prayed for constantly. In the evening after supper, we would—three of us—kneel before a makeshift altar to Our Lady of Lourdes. Silently, Jacques and I would listen as Grandmere made her petition for the safe return of my father—although she never mentioned my mother—mumbling prayers as she fingered the crystal rosary beads. Each night she performed this ritual, earnestly but calmly, as she was a woman of deep faith from which she seemed to derive an inner peace. I believe also she realized, that with both our parents absent, it was essential to our welfare that she present a strong and steadfast persona. I can see her even now—years later—a tall and ramrod-straight figure, her thick white hair in a bun at the nape of her neck, starkly off-set by her severe black apparel. She eschewed any ornament but looked regal nonetheless as she had the demeanor of a no-nonsense woman of respectable attributes and in complete control of herself. With us—her grandchildren—she was neither severe nor coddling—but rather a center of stability in what was to soon become an ever-changing, chaotic world of daily tumult.

CHAPTER 3

First, mother's letters stopped with no apparent explanation. Then our monthly trip to nearby Beaune was cancelled. Grand-mere gave no reason; but both Jacques and I were disappointed because we not only loved to stroll its narrow, winding alleyways but to also visit its vineyard and distillery where we purchased the best Burgundy wine which Grand-mere allowed us to drink moderately at dinner—a special treat. Its claret tinge excited our imagination and its rich body delighted our unsophisticated tongues. In Beaune much of the joie de vivre involved the making of wine, the tasting of wine, the selling of wine, and the imbibing of wine. On alternate months we'd visit the outdoor market in Arles, a colorful and busy place with all types of freshly caught fish—their beady glass-like eyes peering at us from a bed of crinkly crushed ice. In addition, an array of other seafood delicacies was displayed on long wooden tables for purchase. But Grand-mere, especially after the rationing imposed by the Germans, suggested we catch our own; so, with our wine and a picnic-basket fare prepared before our departure, the three of us would wend our way down to the river bank to savor our lunch, followed by fishing. Although life continued in these fairy tale, idyllic villages along the Rhone, we no longer visited them after the arrival of the invaders. Whatever news Grand-mere was intercepting, she did not share it with us. Then suddenly, fewer and fewer men were seen playing *boules* beneath the leafy shade trees in the grassy square designed for these games. In the afternoons when Jacques, I, my friend Monique and her brother René made our way home from school, we could not help but notice the anxious and worried faces of those older men who had not been conscripted or deported as they huddled around café tables rolling tobacco cigarettes and discussing politics in whispers and undertones. One subsequent morning on our usual walk to school, we observed a few soldiers in drab gray uniforms strolling languidly on our street, then on another street when we returned later in the afternoon, which piqued our curiosity. Life in our area was so mundane and uneventful that, being children, we were interested in any little deviation from normal. Once again when we arrived home, René playfully recited what had become our poetic parting signal, "Adieu, Jeanne Marie, mon amie." Once inside we saw that Grand-mere was discussing with a neighboring farmer some adjustment she wanted made to the exterior shutters flanking the long, vertical windows on both floors of our house. Since their discussion was of little interest to us, we scuttled into the kitchen where we were sure to find some freshly baked treat, on this particular day *calissons,* our favorite small almond shaped pastries. Our flame-colored tabby cat jumped from warming itself by the stone hearth to greet us. As the farmer was leaving, Grandmere introduced him as Monsieur LaCloche and informed us that beginning next week, either Jacques or I would be making trips to his farm, so it was best to accompany him home in his horse cart to learn the route. This too was a bit out of the ordinary, so we were glad to see a new place. Once there, the farmer showed us the horse barn, the cow barn where the milking was done, the disgustingly odiferous pig pen, and then introduced us to his wife, Madame LaCloche who at that moment was churning butter. Greeting us warmly, she ceased her labor and invited us to sit at her sturdy oak table covered with a lovely hand-made print cloth of typical Provençal colors—buttercup yellow, rich cobalt blue, and a splash of burnt orange. For the second time in an hour, we feasted on another delectable snack, this time a buttery croissant oozing with home-made purple plum jam. After we thanked her for her graciousness as we had been taught, the farmer pointed out a shorter way home through the woods adjacent to his property but cautioned us to take this path only in daylight since after dusk, it became a confusing maze that would cause us to lose our direction. Again, I thanked him; but Jacques, being a boy and needing to demonstrate his bravado, made a grunt and waved off the admonition.

Chapter 4

efore long, the Germans descended like a black cloud upon our province, bringing with them a human thunderstorm. We began to see more Bosch strutting about in military uniforms, looking sweaty and uncomfortable. Their iron-cleated boots echoed sharply and ominously on the hard-cobbled stone streets. Soon the café/bar at the bottom of Rue Savoir was requisitioned by the Gestapo as their village headquarters. Once the higher-ranking officers arrived, the pleasant and carefree atmosphere in our town drastically changed. People seemed tense, suspicious, edgy and no longer paused on the streets for chatter or casual conversation. As much as possible, neighbors kept close to their homes, mostly indoors. At school we were issued new books—our usual French ones supplemented with German texts.

I did not understand what was happening, but I certainly knew I did **not** like it one bit. I had always been the feistier sibling, and I did not know what Jacques was doing in the adjacent classroom, but I stashed these unfamiliar books beneath my desk. Her own book opened on her desk and repeating the words in unison with Madame and our classmates, Monique glanced at me surreptitiously. Ignoring her as well as Madame's instructions, I chose to be silent. The harsh, guttural sound of the German language assaulted my ears, as would a piece of chalk dragged screeching across a blackboard. My entire psyche rebelled to this onslaught of dissonant consonants and grated me enough to make me shiver. My entire being was poised in rejection, the more so because it had not been my choice to learn it. When class was dismissed, Madame requested I remain; and I must admit my confidence began to wane a bit, but not my sullenness. Monique and René went home without me.

"Jeanne Marie," she began, a concerned look on her face—one that was becoming more common on many in the village. "Why do you not follow the lesson?"

I did not answer at first, because I was not sure of the reason for my defiance. But after some hesitation, I asked my own pointed question, "Why **must** we study from the German books?"

"You are a young girl," she reprimanded although somewhat gently, "and it is not for you to question why."

"Since you are the teacher, isn't it for **YOU** to question why?" I insisted.

"Ah, my dear," she sighed regretfully, "if only I could! It is the 'powers-that-be' who have decided these matters, and we are powerless to refuse."

"Well, **I CHOOSE** to refuse," I retorted vehemently; and with angry, hot tears streaming down my face, fled from the classroom.

Chapter 5

pon my return home, Grand-mere did not notice my rushed entrance as she was busy giving instructions to Monsieur La-Cloche, the farmer, who was doing something with a drill to the long pairs of shutters on each of the windows. Today I was not eager for snacks, friends, or even René's sweet smile. I changed from my school clothes and ran tornado-like out the back door to the cool shade of the woods beyond. Filled with a silent fury entirely foreign to me, I plunged wildly through leafy limbs and thorny briars, over tree stumps, crushing wooden chips and twigs with my stomping feet until, exhausted and spent, I threw myself upon an emerald carpet of sweet-smelling moss. Unable to clearly determine the exact cause of my upset, I just felt some unknown thing gnawing at me. It might have been Madame's words; the insistence on learning the ugly, hateful German; the change in the atmosphere of the village; even Grand-mere's recent unusual silence. And then it occurred to me that what made everything worse was my desire for René's silly poem and sweet good-bye which had always made every afternoon brighter. My heart constricted in my chest at this new awareness. Whatever did it mean? Abruptly I stifled my sobs since I sensed a nearby presence which further incensed me. Even here in the privacy of our own woods, **they** invaded our space as I spied a splendid young German soldier with a pretty lass wearing a white muslin apron as would a milkmaid. They were walking hand-in-hand through this pastoral setting, as I surreptitiously watched, huddled behind the cover of a huge downed log which shielded me. A radiant beam of sunshine sliced through the towering, majestic pines and highlighted the awestruck wonder and naivete` of her angelic face as enraptured, she stood facing him. Vicariously enamored, I observed this romantic scenario, the pale visage of the lass turned upward to the boy—yes, boy—for his upper lip betrayed just a hint of light, fine hair. At that moment leaning down, the lad kissed her expectant lips after which she abruptly, and with a single peal of laughter, turned and ran from him in mirthful teasing. Following her flight, he caught up and gently took her hand again as they wended their way out of the dense foliage toward the edge of the forest to where it abutted the farm pasture. Fat-bellied cows, their udders hanging loosely below, chewed rhythmically on their cud, as if ruminating the problems of the world. Lying breathlessly still crouched and peering from behind a clump of trees, I felt I was witnessing something beautiful, wondrous, almost beatific—in this hallowed, sylvan Eden of towering forest, tangled vines, and creeping ground cover. Hummingbirds soared upward toward the penetrating light steaming through the spires of trees. An innocent adolescent, inexperienced and ignorant of the adult ways of the world, I was entranced by what had just occurred between the young couple; it transcended all earthly experiences of my own. It was as if Heaven in all its brilliant glory pierced the ebony darkness of the dense foliage to shine its light on pure love, if that was indeed what I interpreted through the couple's sweetly gentle interaction. Attributing a sanctity I had never before ascribed to this tranquil natural haven, I allowed myself to be imbued with its inner peace and serenity, completely freeing me of all that day's angst with which I had entered the woods.

CHAPTER 6

Upon my return home, I anticipated a scolding from my grandmother since it was almost dusk. But instead Grand-mere was assiduously examining the shutters as she worked them back and forth—open-close, open-close, open-close. Apparently satisfied, she seemed to be peering downward from our perch on the hill toward the bottom of Rue Savoir where the German headquarters had replaced the often-frequented, popular café. As a result of Grand-mere's preoccupation with the wooden blinds, I was able to make my way silently upstairs to wash off the grass stains and tend to the scratches from the tangled briars that had grabbed at me in my flight through the forest. Upon my descent from the upper floor, I saw that the table had been set for dinner. In the center were some provisions my brother Jacques had procured the previous day from farmer LaCloche—a hunk of aged cheese, supplemented by a very small loaf of crusty bread, and a few root vegetables simmered in broth which served as a type of soup. Before the occupation, we had an abundance of delectable delicacies like warm stewed figs and strawberries, pan-fried strips of foie gras, but alas, no more. Since the constraints imposed by the occupiers on food purchases, Jacques had been making more frequent trips to Monsieur LaCloche's farm. Many of the staples we formerly had in abundance became difficult to obtain—sugar, flour—meat was a rarity. Some obtained these goods on the black market, but that was dangerous since neighbors now spied on neighbors, an abhorrence unheard of before now. Some villagers had become members of the elite Gestapo in an effort to protect themselves and be in good graces with their captors. It was relatively easy to identify these traitors since they were always well-dressed—formal suits and hats—without the lean and hungry look of the average townsfolk. But as rations were issued, rules became strictly enforced and conditions deteriorated; supplies of every kind became scarcer and scarcer so that all were desperate, and no one was to be trusted. It was rumored that in the larger cities people were starving, chaos prevailed, and even that certain groups of people—Jews specifically—were being evicted from their homes and herded into ghettos. Many found that hard to believe, for the Jewish merchants and bankers centered in the cities had always exercised the power that came with having money. But more and more news of persecution sifted through daily—Jewish establishments and businesses were attacked and destroyed, beating the owners who tried to intervene, looting and burning the store's contents in the streets. There were very few Jews living in the countryside since most owned businesses and made their living in urban locations; but there were a few: the Levines, the Lowensteins, the Lewinskys. I had noticed that the children of these local families no longer attended school, had wondered why, and asked the newly-assigned teacher who had replaced Madame Hugot. Curtly, I was told to "mind my own business"—that "it was none of my affair" which allowed no further inquiry. I wondered when things would go back to the relaxed and pleasant way they had been before, and I often brooded about the pall that hung over daily life. Grandmere said that we were lucky to have our home to ourselves—many had been seized by the Germans for sequestering their own troops so that other less fortunate families were relegated to a single room or two while the detested occupiers made themselves at home in others' quarters. Such was the case with the Chars—Monique and René had been displaced to a claustrophobic attic-alcove while German soldiers slept comfortably in the children's former commodious bedrooms. Initially, their father had vociferously protested until he was silenced by threats of transport to the labor camps from which no one ever returned. A heavy somberness hung over everything, and life as we once knew it was suspended in time. We all lived in a type of limbo unaware that some not so far away had already been dispersed to hell.

Chapter 7

Grand-mere seemed to be preparing for something although I could not have imagined what. She appeared to move with purpose. One day after my return from school, Grand-mere invited me to join her at the table, poured herself a cup of ersatz coffee—a blend of chicory and something else—since real coffee was not to be had—then heated some milk. Placing the mug of steaming milk before me, she sat, then reached out to lovingly place one hand upon my arm as she reached with the other for her cup of coffee. She had placed towels beneath front and back doorways to block the aroma since if recognized, it would attract unwanted visitors who would want to know where we procured it.

"Ma chere," she began, "you have always been a most observant and mature girl, so you must be confused about some of the recent events. Do you wish to tell me how you are feeling?"

"Bonne-maman, why do people look so frightened and why are the German soldiers **here**? Since they've come, everything is vastly different. People remain indoors, hiding behind their walls. On the streets they almost run instead of walk—and always look down. I **want** these Krauts to leave!" I nearly shouted in a high-pitched, shrill voice, as her face contorted in displeasure.

Grand-mere made no attempt to stifle my honest expression of distress. This conversation was probably long overdue, but she had wanted to shield us as long as she could. Now that was no longer possible. More German military appeared in the town each day expanding their demands, ordering residents to relinquish whatever possessions the soldiers fancied or needed, and imposing evening curfews. One of the worst was being coerced to share living quarters with these rude and over-bearing strangers who had invaded the residents' privacy and family life. As food became scarcer, they resented the necessity of dividing what little they had with these crude and vulgar barbarians. However, all had to admit that the higher-ranking officers who arrived daily were more refined—some even bordering on polite—a couple of those in command seemingly embarrassed and apologizing for the intrusion. But make no mistake, beneath their more gentlemanly facade, we were aware that they too had to follow orders from Berlin; and we existed in trepidation never knowing what additional sacrifices those orders might entail.

I knew Grand-mere was pondering how to explain these complex political developments to me—a willful child—without further arousing my ire and frustration. Her priority always was to keep you—in my case, to keep me—safe from myself since my emotions tended to run high; and unlike my grandmother who had years of practice stoically accepting what vicissitudes life had dealt her, I had yet to learn to mask and keep my feelings in check. Before her dismissal, Madame Hugot had visited Grand-mere to share her discomfit with my unwillingness to comply with the use of the German school texts recently issued. She was concerned that I might bring negative attention to myself with dire results. For my own sake, Grand-mere could no longer delay taking control of the situation by issuing warnings and explaining as best she could why recalcitrance could be dangerous. Nevertheless, she allowed me to vent privately to her for fear that I might explode in front of the wrong person.

"Ma chere, please listen intently. These are turbulent times. We are no longer free to do as we would like. Presently the Germans are our conquerors, and so we must obey their orders. But they will not always be in control, though you must not be heard expressing this desire for their defeat. I assure you, just as day follows night and spring follows winter, this too will change. Our job is to simply keep faith, accept this temporary cross, and hold fast to hope for a better day. Do you hear me, Jeanne Marie? Do you understand what I am telling you?"

Mulling over her words. I remained silent for some time. I wanted to protest—was struggling not to. Peering across the table to take in Grand-mere's countenance, I noticed a new guardedness never there before, a vulnerability she had never allowed to show. Her lips had developed a downward curve, but her voice was ever strong and determined. She **would not be vanquished;** she would protect me and Jacques who were in her charge. It was her sacred duty.

Standing to firmly embrace me from behind as I sat sullenly in the straight-backed kitchen chair at the table, she leaned over me and whispered against my ear, "You must be patient and offer all these sufferings and indignities to God in preparation for the day that we will be delivered from this evil. I assure you He hears our prayers for strength to endure this for now. You need only trust that a better day will come."

Brushing her cheek against the top of my head, Bonne-maman seemed to be savoring its silky texture upon which she often remarked. Cupping my cheeks, which she frequently said looked too pale, she planted a gentle kiss upon my head as if in blessing. "May God keep this beautiful and innocent child safely in the palm of His hand," she prayed.

CHAPTER 8

One day just as we had suspected might happen, we were summoned by a hard series of raps upon the door. When I moved to answer it, Grand-mere instructed me to exit quietly by the back door and secret myself in the woods that edged the property until the departure of the visitor.

Boldly approaching the door and holding herself erect so as to emphasize her full height, Grand-mere opened it with a wide full swing. No timid, fearful shrinking or quivering voice greeted the German officer.

"Bonjour, Madame Molineau. I am Lt. Eric Schrader, assigned to oversee your lovely town. May I come in?" Stepping aside, Grand-mere waved her arm as if to invite him inside the wide foyer. Ahead of him toward the back, a winding staircase with a satin mahogany curved balustrade led to the upper floor.

"Excusez-moi. I hope I am not disturbing you, but I have an errand of importance," he prefaced his request.

"No," Grand-mere responded. "It is quite all right, but may I inquire as to your business?"

"Well, regrettably my commanding officer, Col. Hartz, is due to arrive tomorrow, and I must arrange housing for him. Oh, forgive me. Please pardon my slip. I do not mean to suggest that I regret his arrival; only that it necessitates my imposing upon you. I have observed your handsome residence perched upon this hill looking down upon our headquarters at the bottom of the street. I must say that it looked very inviting from the exterior, and now I see that it is equally well-appointed inside."

Realistically Grand-mere had been anticipating this moment for some time, and she was prepared. It helped that her height matched his so that she dared to look him fully, directly in the face, her steely blue eyes boring into his, rather than retreating or averting her gaze. He seemed impressed by her confidence and elegant poise which suggested the noble background of a superior in class and breeding,

"So, may I inquire as to your purpose here in my home?" she ventured to ask. "If it is to requisition my home for the colonel, I must tell you that I am raising two grand-children here who can be rambunctious at times, playful and energetic as all children, but noisy and often silly with their games. There is only so much one can do to control the high spirits and hijinks of robust and curious children. In addition, they can sometimes be quarrelsome. The colonel might not appreciate your choice of a place for him that might not be conducive to the quiet, rest, and relaxation he might desire."

The handsome and courtly lieutenant could have clearly demanded that Grand-mere accommodate the colonel, but she seemed to have gained the upper hand. He did not even ask the age of the children. Perhaps he was unaccustomed to dealing with strong and determined females, or perhaps he was too much of a gentleman to force the issue. It may also have been his concern that the colonel would hold him responsible if unable to enjoy peace and quiet in this residence. Whatever the case, he had met his match and chose not to pursue his purpose further. Unaware of the background of this imperious woman, her status or connections, this young underling had allowed himself to be intimidated.

Lt. Schrader simply tipped his hat, thanked Madame for the information, turned, clicked his heels, and departed without further ado. She was only too cognizant that luck had been on her side this time. An older, more experienced officer or one not so malleable could easily have scoffed at her weak argument, put her out on the street with no roof above her head. Although she had maintained her composure, it had taken every ounce of her willpower; and following the officer's departure, Grand-mere retreated to the kitchen, hands shaking, body trembling from the strain, and slumped into the nearest chair.

"Mon Dieu! Thank God the children are not here to witness this collapse," she lamented to herself.

CHAPTER 9

Three days later, we were awakened by shouting from the street which summoned us to our bedroom windows. Through the peep-holes Monsieur LaCloche had drilled into the shutters, we could see to the bottom of Rue Savoir where a man, bloodied and curled into a fetal position, was being kicked viciously and repeatedly. With each pointed thrust from the officer's shiny, ebony boot, the victim's body jolted, rolling over and over again, until it lay lifeless on the other side of the street. As if to assure that the pedestrian would not ever rise again, the vicious final blow was delivered with a rifle butt that fractured the skull with an audible crack. Sickening lines of deep crimson life-blood trickled from the man's orifices—ears, nose, mouth—darkly staining the street and streaming languidly into the gutter. For the horrified onlookers, the entire scene transpired in slow motion. Never before had we witnessed such uncivilized brutality. From his bedroom window, Jacques was unaware that his tightly balled fists had turned his knuckles white. From my bedroom window, I stared in awestruck disbelief, my hands clenched over my trembling mouth to stifle the screams I so vehemently forced myself to swallow, so that my chest ached in actual physical pain. In shock, gasping for breath, I retreated behind the long draperies pooling on the hardwood floor. Immediately following the attack, the medal-bedecked officer sputtered staccato orders to two soldiers standing wooden-like nearby. *"Unterscharfuhrer, rechts!"* (Sergeant, to the right). *"Schneller"* (Hurry up). Coming alive, jumping into action, the pair hastily and roughly performed the final indignity to the deceased. The taller of the two grasped the limp hands, the shorter one his twisted feet, and together—in unison—dragged the lifeless corpse toward the right to a wooden cart into which they dumped him unceremoniously.

"Heim!" bellowed the colonel. Upon that order, a couple of incredulous onlookers, who had risen early, dispersed and returned to their homes.

From the parlor window, Grand-mere, who always rose at the crack of dawn, knew we—Jacques and I—were viewing this horrible spectacle from the upper story. I imagined her cringing, hunched forward to realize that this nightmare would be eternally singed in our memories.

When I descended the staircase clutching the rail as if for balance, Jacques just behind me, we gaped speechless at our grandmother. Sensing that no words could suffice to assuage our shock, she approached us, then swept us tightly into a wide embrace. Impotent with grief, helplessness, and rage, all she could do to comfort her precious grand-children was to embrace us in her outstretched arms. We remained like that a long time, a tableau of incomprehensible misery, until she gently kissed me, then my brother, taking our hands, one in each of hers, and led us away from the front room.

The brilliant tangerine sun, so cherished in the Provençal countryside for its ability to create the unique light cherished by the most skilled artists, still cast its dazzling glow onto Rue Savoir. On this day in 1942, it streamed brilliantly through the glass panes of the tall pairs of vertical windows symmetrically flanking the front portal. Reflecting the hues of the antique, stained-glass shade of a lamp upon a rosewood end-table, this fiery orb spattered gorgeous gules of color onto the wide planked floor boards, creating a natural mosaic of verdant greens, vibrant yellows, and cobalt blues. We sat in communion as a family attempting to digest a simple breakfast after the inhumane barbarism we had just witnessed; while outside the heat of that same celestial globe dried and baked into the cobblestones another mosaic—this one ugly and detestable, of various grotesque crimson hues—streaked magenta, blackish-purple—scorched into the uneven cobblestones at the bottom of Rue Savoir. Although by end of day, the Germans would wash away the vestiges of this assault on an innocent victim, **NEVER** could the psyches of those who witnessed it be cleansed of the black memory of desecration in this place of stark beauty and pure light.

Part II

A Heavy Darkness Overshadows the Provençal Countryside

CHAPTER 10

Since the colonel had arrived, conditions deteriorated for the villagers. The few adult men who had somehow escaped notice—even those with disabilities—were rounded up and transported to work camps. Even some females were seen fit for hard labor, leaving only children, old men, and women who were terrorized with rising frequency. One frail and elderly man basking idly in the luxurious warmth of the mid-day sun, his crinkled eyes at half mast, found his chair kicked from under him, the unfortunate scapegoat of the irascible colonel who randomly chose this harmless individual upon whom to vent his anger at that moment. Following their superior's example, or fearful that he would deem them too lenient, his military underlings, formerly mild in their harassment of the villagers, became more hostile and insulting. From behind her closed shutters, Grand-mere saw all. Observing the severe demeanor of the colonel, she knew that had he visited her rather than the easily dissuaded lieutenant, she would not be standing here in her own house.

Monsieur LaCloche was no longer summoned since he had completed all modifications to the house per Grand-mere's instructions which included embellishing a wall with decorative panels which Grand-mere ordered Jacques repaint. The boy wondered why Grand-mere bothered with such frivolity at a time like this; but when he asked, Grand-mere was vague—something about needing a change—a lift—especially at times of such restriction when the only thing that was still under her control was her property, and "who knows when that will change." Feeling clever and witty, hoping to impress her with his scant knowledge of English derived from a British vacationer the previous summer, the teenager teasingly recited a line he remembered from their reading of the poem "The Charge of the Light Brigade." Taking up the paintbrush and dipping it in the bucket, Jacques grinned teasingly and translated with a sardonic smirk: "Ours not to make reply. Ours not to reason why. Ours but to do and die." To his utter astonishment, his grandmother appeared stricken and paled.

CHAPTER 11

Jeanne Marie began to notice that her brother was frequently absent from school. Rather than worry Grand-mere about his whereabouts, she confronted Jacques directly.

"I don't want to tattle-tale about your skipping school lately, but where do you go when you are not in attendance? I worry for your safety with all that is going on around here. The Gestapo is getting stricter and stricter about enforcing rules. Just last week…"

"Just last week," Jacques mimicked her. "Just last week they imposed a curfew and cut our food rations again," he replied bitterly. "Haven't you noticed that Grand-mere is struggling to feed us. So, I spend time at Farmer LaCloche's helping him with the chores in return for milk, butter, and eggs so that Grand-mere doesn't need to buy them. THERE! OK?"

"I'm sorry. I didn't know," his sister apologized, chagrined.

"There are **more important** things to do than reading those stupid German text books they forced upon us!"

"I know," she agreed, "I hate them too."

"Hey, are you being bothered by the Krauts on your way to school? Is that why you are asking? Doesn't Monique and that simpleton René walk with you each day? The way he looks at you!! Why that fool is crazy for you."

"Don't be cruel," his sister scolded. "I'm glad to have their company, especially since **you** are nowhere to be found."

"Then **what** do you need me for?"

"Oh, Jacques, I feel danger everywhere even if I have not personally attracted attention. So many people appear on edge all the time. The Lowensteins and another Jewish family disappeared in the middle of the night. When we asked the new teacher about their whereabouts, she dismissed our questions. No one knows where they went. It is said that in the cities Jews have been rounded up and relocated, but no one quite knows what to believe. There are rumors…"

"Yes, **I** have heard them too," Jacques interrupted her, as if afraid of where she was going with this. "That is why I have been helping Farmer LaCloche. We **can't just wait and see!**"

"What do you mean?" Jeanne Marie asked puzzled. "Wait for what? What are you helping him with?" She persisted.

"I **told** you," he retorted. "with the farm chores.

"Oh," she replied chastised, "it sounded like you were helping him with something else."

"Look," continued her brother, regretting that he had mentioned Farmer LaCloche at all. "Don't concern yourself with me and what I am doing. Be a good girl. Go to school. Learn your lessons but stick with René and Monique. There's safety in numbers."

"Not anymore," she retorted. "People are not safe anymore. What about that poor old man…"

Again, Jacques interrupted her. His face was flushed. "**Don't** remind me," he was shouting now, and his countenance was distorted in an ugly grimace. "I don't want to hear anymore."

Jeanne began to cry. She had never seen her brother like this. "I'm just afraid," she confessed.

"That is why **we are doing what needs to be done!**" Jacques asserted.

"What does **that** mean? Who are '**we**' and '**what**' are you doing?"

"Not to worry. The less you know the better. But don't go fretting to Grand-mere about me. That would accomplish nothing." Then he leaned down and kissed her gently on the cheek.

What his sister could not possibly imagine was that Jacques was part of MUR, Mouvement de Resistance, a freedom fighter who had trekked to nearby Aix-en-Provence, considered the most picturesque village, a site of beauty and culture. However, there was a dark side. In the lovely town of Les Milles, the German occupiers, with the help of the Vichy government, had taken over a brickworks factory and converted it into an internment camp for artists, writers and other intellectuals who opposed Fascism. As a result, they were considered undesirable by the Wehrmacht because some had been involved in publishing anti-Nazi writings. The camp was a hellish place of filth and

vermin. Most captives suffered from nagging respiratory prob-
lems, breathing in brick dust and coughing up blood. From afar,
Jacques had observed this with his own eyes, and had, with the
help of other underground saboteurs, assisted one escapee smug-
gled out while disguised as a woman. Once beyond camp bound-
aries, they guided him to Bayonne on the southwest coast where
their contacts would take over and get him by sea to a safe haven.
That was the meaning of his retort to Jeanne, "We are doing what
needs to be done!"

Jacques was constantly on the move, although his sister
could not have imagined the extent of his clandestine efforts to
thwart the abhorred Bosch. She only knew that he was going to
church frequently. She surmised that perhaps the worse things
got, the more he prayed for their deliverance. Grand-mere would
certainly have approved of this new-found religious devotion.
But very late one evening, she stealthily followed him, too curious
to know what he was up to. Aware that this was dangerous since
it was beyond the curfew the Germans had imposed, she nonetheless trailed her brother into the dark woods, keeping some distance behind. Once in the cover of the grove, she crouched low to
avoid dangling branches, almost crawling through particularly
dense sections. Reaching the deepest, thickest part of the forest,
she observed that Jacques stopped, stood deathly still, scanning
all around him, ears and eyes pricked for any intruder. When assured that it was safe, he began dismantling something which
Jeanne Marie could not discern clearly. At first it appeared that
one of the plane trees had partly fallen, as it was lying slanted at
an angle. But with each leafy branch Jacques lifted, she saw a tiny
hut emerge. So skillfully covered and camouflaged by tree limbs,
it just blended into the greenery of the woods. Two figures

emerged from the tiny structure and helped him rearrange the cover. Then he led them to the edge of the forest, creeping through underbrush, as did Jeanne Marie, her heart hammering in her chest as she realized how risky her brother's actions. Ominous wispy, gray shadows intermingled and hovered at every turn. To her amazement, Jacques brought his charges to the back of the village church where someone silently motioned them inside. What she could not have guessed was that with the help of the Catholic priest, Jacques had devised a hiding space between the organ pipes and beneath the floor boards. Fleeing Jews were hidden there until such time as it was safe to help them reach the foothills of the Pyrenees and hopefully over into Spain. Having learned the reason for Jacques' audacious nocturnal wanderings, his sister crept home and crawled into bed, praying that the night would blot out her brother's covert activities.

CHAPTER 12

Very late one night, there was a frantic pounding on the back door. All three—Grand-mere, Jeanne, and Jacques—were awakened by the knocking.

"Remain here," Grand-mere instructed. Jeanne Marie obeyed, glued to the floor; but Jacques ran ahead of his grandmother to the door.

Hesitating before allowing entry, together they inquired, "Who's there? What do you want?"

"PLEASE HELP! HELP, I BEG YOU. OPEN THE DOOR!" was the panicked plea in between heaving sobs.

It was Jacques who opened the door to see a bedraggled woman huddled in the doorway clutching a child. Her *chemise de nuit* was muddy, and the child was lethargic. Both were scraped and bruised.

"Oh, mon Dieu," whispered the hysterical mother. "They have taken my husband—my dear, good *mari*—who did no wrong. Why? Why are we so persecuted? They arrested him because he brought us food—me and our ailing child."

"What do you mean?" Grand-mere reached out to embrace the small *enfant* wrapped in a ragged blanket and hugged it to her breast.

"We could not register for the rations. We are Jews and have been starving so my husband, Monsieur Levine, traded his gold wedding band for food on the black market. Someone must have followed him … reported him." It took all her strength for Mrs. Levine to spit out this information before she totally lost her composure, falling in a heaving thud upon the floor.

Jeanne Marie had managed to stifle her anxiety and approached them warily. Even the ginger-striped tabby cat looked on curiously, the v-shaped mark on its forehead peaked in a quizzical stare, his tail kinked in a question mark. As Grand-mere passed the silent child to Jeanne, she enveloped the weeping mother in her arms and coaxed her toward the sofa.

"Calm yourself," she soothed. "You are safe with us for now. You must rest, and the child must eat. *Demain* (tomorrow) we can find out about your husband."

"Merci. Merci," cried Mrs. Levine. "Merci. Merci," she kept repeating mindlessly.

"Jeanne Marie, heat some milk. Jacques, find some bread and cheese. Do not light any candles or lanterns. No one must see any activity here," Grand-mere instructed.

After feeding and calming mother and child, they were put to bed upstairs. Once settled and sleeping restlessly after their ordeal, Grand-mere gathered Jeanne and Jacques in the kitchen.

"We can shield them here for only so long," whispered Grand-mere regretfully. "We must have a plan."

"I already have a plan," offered Jacques confidently.

"Whatever do you mean?" queried his grandmother.

"I cannot tell you," he replied. "Tomorrow I will take care of it. You will see."

His grand-mother tightened her shawl around her chest. Incredulous, Jeanne stared at her brother. Only now did some of his earlier remarks make sense, although she could not guess what he was planning. What had he said? "I can't just wait and see." Hadn't those been his words?

With this decision, Jacques seemed to have grown up overnight. Grand-mere had missed the signs of his maturing. Partly it frightened her and partly it relieved her to have some assistance in this most urgent matter which had fallen on her doorstep. But she harbored a foreboding that this might be only the first step in her grandson taking matters into his own hands. She saw him as only a boy—a mere *garcon*; but just a few months shy of fifteen, he was approaching adulthood—soon to become a man. Right now, boys just a bit older were fighting and dying on the battlefields which sobered and terrified her. She could not allow her thoughts to wander there, for that would be her undoing. She must only concentrate on the present moment—the here and now; and if Jacques—a young MAN now, could help in this situation, she must allow him sway—in fact, she must allow him to take the lead.

CHAPTER 13

Jacques was already gone when Mrs. Levine and her child awakened late the next day. Exhausted with worry and fear, they had slept into the afternoon. Grand-mere made sure that all was quiet so as not to disturb them. She had sent Jeanne off to school with her friends; nothing must seem amiss. Mrs. Levine appeared to be in a daze, almost as if she remembered the previous day as a terrible nightmare—even talking of going home to see if her husband had returned. Rather than contradict or upset her further, Grand-mere comforted the distraught woman as she served breakfast—or rather lunch—given the late hour of their rising. Ms. Levine kept rambling about rumors she had heard—that in the camps, the breasts of new mothers were taped causing them to swell with unused milk, restricted from feeding their babies. In agony and pain, they had to watch their little ones starving to death. Their sinister captors seemed to be measuring the endurance of both mother and child in a type of diabolical experiment. Grand-mere tried to conceal her horror at this news so as not to further feed Madame Levine's panic. The woman kept babbling on, sometimes hysterically incoherent—about political prisoners in Fresnes interrogated mercilessly during a type of water-torture where, in bathtubs requisitioned from Jewish homes, the victim's head was held under freezing water to the point of drowning. Grand-mere kept the long shutters drawn and kept to the back of the house. Judging both mother and child would feel more civilized in fresh, clean clothes following a bath, she heated water, then filled the tub, although at first, Madame Levine shivered when she glanced at it. Upstairs Grand-mere found a dress and sweater of her own for Mrs. Levine and for the child some used, but freshly laundered clothes, from when Jeanne Marie was small. In addition, she brought down some lavender water which she dropped into the tub because it was one of her own small pleasures, the familiar scent of the Provençal countryside. Its essence always seemed to lift her spirits, providing her with a sense of home, since this purple flower grew prolifically in the bucolic landscape with which she was blessed to be surrounded. She knew that the Levines' respite in her home was only temporary; but she would do all in her power to strengthen them, help them heal, before giving them up to continue their journey. Before he left, Jacques had assured her that he would lead them to another safe-haven; and he brooked no interference. Silently she offered thanks to God for this unexpected blessing in the guise of her grandson, although in expressing her gratitude to the Father, she was bothered by a niggling sense of unworthiness, which she tried to brush away. She was only too aware of the one sin for which she felt onerous guilt, and she wondered if her kindness to these strangers might be a subconscious attempt to atone after all this time. With this uneasy thought preying on her mind, she dozed until Jeanne Marie returned from school.

Part III

FURTHER DANGEROUS EXPLOITS

[HAPTER 14

f course, Jacques had not been attending school although Grand-mere did not know this. Instead he had been with farmer LaCloche. Returning home with some provisions, he told Grand-mere that he had found a place for Mrs. Levine and her child and would transport them the next night under cover of darkness. Grand-mere knew enough to ask no questions while Jacques took Mrs. Levine aside and spoke to her privately. She became agitated at some point because Grand-mere could discern her repeating Monsieur Levine's name in a high-pitched, plaintive voice; but Jacques managed to quiet her with reassurances. After an uneventful evening of fitful napping, eating, resting, they arose a couple of hours before dawn, quickly dressed in warm, dark clothing and headed for the back door with Jacques in the lead. Grand-mere hugged Mrs. Levine, then the child to her breast, kissed them on both cheeks, and wished them God-speed. While Jeanne Marie looked on sleepily, she was well aware of the danger to all of them should they be intercepted. When they had gone, Grand-mere took the girl in her arms and led her to the shrine in her bedroom.

"Ma belle petite-fille," she soothed. "All we can do now is pray. Pray for them, for Jacques' safe return, for my dearest son (your father), and for your mother."

Jeanne Marie was taken aback since Grand-mere had rarely, if ever, mentioned her mother other than announcing that her letters had ceased to arrive. It seemed to Jeanne, that **that** was when they should have begun praying for her mother; but Grand-mere's tone had been hard to read. Something in her voice seemed to allow no inquiry. Well, that wasn't it exactly. Both Jacques and Jeanne had sensed that this was a subject off limits. Although Grand-mere had **never** voiced her feelings about their mother, the absence of any mention of her puzzled them. Actually, they had never heard their grandmother disparage or speak ill of anyone, including their mother. It was just the total absence of their mother's name that seemed strange given Grand-mere's charac-teristic kindness, charity, and good-will to all. Whatever the case, on this particular night they included in their prayers the name "Cecille." Just the sound of her mother's name warmed Jeanne Marie beyond all else. She spoke the name "Cecille" in a reveren-tial tone, acutely aware how much she missed her. **WHERE** was she? **HOW** was she? **WHY** had her correspondence stopped? All these unknowns had torn at Jeanne Marie for so long without any answers. With the mention of that name "Cecille," it was as if a dam had finally given way and a deluge of emotion, like a powerful, cathartic waterfall, cascaded like a flood. Grand-mere rocked her granddaughter in her arms as their tears blended together.

CHAPTER 15

Jacques led his charges through the dense woods, their trepidation nearly palpable. He had waited till just before dawn because although he knew the forest in and out, he preferred a bit of daylight to make the trek easier on them. Arriving at La-Cloche's, Jacques ushered them into the barn where the farmer was already milking the cows. Startled, the farmer jumped when they entered; but as Jacques explained their precarious situation, LaCloche discontinued the milking and went into the house returning with hot ersatz coffee for the woman, warm milk for the child, and buttered rolls with a bit of sausage. Then he and Jacques went about showing them their "quarters." When Jacques should have been at school these past weeks, he had been here with La-Cloche constructing what appeared to be a large, rectangular cistern for collecting rain water. But both the boy and the man had been preparing for such a moment as this. Together they had indeed created a cistern, but at its top had built a deep shelf which they filled with brackish water. The bottom half, however, remained empty space which reached below ground level into a dug-out cavity. If anyone were to lift the lid peering into the construction from the top, it appeared to be filled with water. The hollow space which extended from beneath the shelf into a dug-out trench below was designed to serve as a hiding space. It was into this that mother and child were secreted. Although the weather was still mild, they could remain here only temporarily. The next step would be to secure transport to a safer place. Once the Levines were settled, Jacques went on his way—not to school but to a secret rendezvous. He was not finished with outwitting the Huns on this particular day. In fact, **this** was all he lived for now. **This** was his renewed purpose, and he would not flinch nor cower. He experienced a thrill each time he thwarted this detestable enemy. He would retaliate against these arrogant interlopers with his brain rather than with a gun. The mind was a powerful weapon when exercised cleverly, and he had every intention of doing just that for the abasement the villagers had suffered under the German command. He had begun to realize the fragility of freedom and believed the Resistance took its noblest form in the simple acts of good people like his grand-mere and others like himself, members of a band known as "Maquis," the collective name given to partisans fighting the German invaders. The bravest and most illustrious of freedom fighters was Jean Moulin who had recently been taken prisoner and after months of torture died on a transport train. When Jacques heard of the demise of these heroes he admired so, his heart constricted in rage and fury. His raw emotion was exacerbated by the overt collaboration of the Vichy government—Frenchmen themselves—with the SS and Gestapo—the most despicable, abhorrent traitors who turned on their own. These facts made him all the more determined to sabotage the iron-fisted enemy no matter the personal cost. Yes, it was perilous work he performed; but these were extraordinary times which required ordinary people like himself to rise and summon the inner strength and courage they never knew they possessed.

CHAPTER 16

René was no longer coming with his sister Monique to accompany Jeanne Marie to school. In fact, he was, like Jacques, frequently absent. Jeanne hated to admit that she missed his shy attentions to her. Previously she had thought his fawning a bit silly—even irritating, but now she wished he were here. Often lately she was confused by what she saw, how she felt, by life in general. Everything had been turned upside down— tipsy-turvy—off kilter. The general unease surrounding her put her nerves on edge. If this sense of displacement were not bad enough, it became more specific when the colonel made a visit to Grand-mere one Saturday. Not even bothering to knock, he barged in fuming, demanding to know where Jacques was.

Despite the colonel's glaring countenance, Grand-mere re-tained her regal demeanor—dignified, calm, and controlled—not giving him the satisfaction of seeing someone tremble under his threatening scowl.

"What is **this**?" she responded to the rude intrusion. She felt she was walking on a tight-rope, uncertain as to how taut she could stretch it. His glowering visage warned her to be careful.

'It has been brought to my attention that your grandson has become a person of interest."

"A 'person of interest'?" repeated Grand-mere. "What kind of interest would anyone have in a mere boy?"

"Need I remind you, Madame Molineau, that he is hardly a boy. Some of his age are already at the front fighting for the fa-therland."

It occurred to Grand-mere that what he was referring to was **not** her fatherland, but she bit her tongue. She had no inten-tion of making things any worse; and this crass, vile Hun was after her beloved Jacques.

"Why, I don't know," she responded cautiously.

"**Don't be coy with me**," he thundered, hoping to unsettle her composure. **"I am not so easily duped as the lieutenant."**

Jeanne Marie stood stark still in the background, stricken with terror, her heart pulsing in her throat, tears welling in her eyes.

"Well then, maybe the girl knows," he turned to Jeanne who blanched, flinching before his terrifying countenance, return-ing his glare with stony silence.

"**COLONEL**," bellowed Grand-mere, "what is the mean-ing of attacking an innocent child? We have done nothing to deserve this. We are law-abiding, noble French citizens graciously accepting defeat. What more can you desire of us?"

"Madame, I am aware of your deceit. You will recall Lt. Schrader's earlier visit before my arrival. He was told this house—so convenient for my lodging because it was so near to my head-quarters below—was, however, not acceptable."

With this the colonel approached the window, drew back the curtain, pointing directly to the foot of our street. "When I inquired of Lt. Schrader why he had not considered it, he said, of course, he had but was dissuaded by Madame who said there were noisy, young children. **Is <u>SHE</u>—standing there stupidly— one of those noisy children to whom you referred. Why, she looks like an** *imbecile*—**as if she's lost her tongue as well as her sense! And your grandson—what is his name—Jacques, I believe, is he another? You seem, Madame Molineau, to be a coddling grand-mama too reluctant to pull the tit from out their suckling gums!!!"**

"**How dare you!**" shrieked Grand-mere in a strident voice, rising to her full height, her straight posture still impeccable. "You dishonor yourself and your country with such crude insults, bullying an old, defenseless woman. I repeat, we are upright, loyal, noble French citizens—proudly Gallic to the core—and surely you know your behavior is **shameful. I repeat. You dishonor yourself, as well as your country!** Do you believe your superiors would condone this **crude, unseemly** language?" Chastised, his face reddened. She had successfully hit her mark.

Jeanne-Marie—agape—in shock, could not fathom how Grand-mere held her ground—stately, undaunted in her defiance. But Madame Molineau would **never, never cower before this crass brute** despite his ferocious stare. She would **never** succumb to these Teutonic barbarians, uncouth interlopers of her land, her home, her country, this idyllic retreat—her beloved France, considered the epitome of culture the world over.

As if reading her mind, the colonel turned abruptly on his heel, slamming the door as he departed with a loud clicking of his heels, the sound reverberating like a gunshot. Grand-mere remained rigid and still for what seemed to Jeanne an eternity. Then the girl ran to her grandmother, throwing herself wildly into her safe embrace.

PART IV

UNSPEAKABLE TRAGEDY

CHAPTER 17

Jacques did not return that night, nor the next. Grand-mere sent me to Farmer LaCloche to see if he had been working there, but he had not.

We remained in limbo and prayed all the more fervently for his safe return, as well as Papa's—and for my mother too. If only we would get some news.

Then suddenly late one afternoon, unexpectedly René came bursting through the back door, babbling something about Jacques and **hiding, hiding, hiding.** We asked if Jacques was hiding somewhere. Why was he hiding? Where? But rather than answering us, René appeared wild, delirious, saying, "**Me! Me! Me! I must hide. The Bosch! They will come. They are after us.**"

Both fearful and perplexed, Grand-mere led him through the hall to the wall recently painted reluctantly by Jacques after Farmer LaCloche's carpentry alterations. She removed a molding and prodded him inside the narrow slit that appeared.

"You must remain upright—standing," instructed Grand-mere in a tremulous voice. "Not a sound. Do you hear me? Can you do it? It is so tight in there." She did not wait for a response but snapped on the molding to cover the aperture. No sooner was he positioned, someone else came pounding at the door.

"Mon Dieu," lamented Grand-mere, as she responded to the shouts outside. A neighbor woman was wailing, screaming, crying, babbling—followed quickly by another at her heels.

"O-o-o-h! Madame. Come quick! Come quick! Alas! Alas! My God! Mon Dieu!"

Frantic, Grand-mere and I followed them. Running. Racing. Tripping. Our breath coming in short, sharp gasps. I had a painful stitch in my side. More joined us as we followed the original frantic messenger who was waving her hands in the air like a dervish. Ahead was an enclosed outdoor space, open only on one side where the men used to play *boules*. A crowd had already assembled there so Grand-mere and I could not see the interior. Upon recognizing Grand-mere, they opened a path for us.

My heart stopped! My blood ran cold! My stomach churned. My head throbbed. I could not breathe! Felt dizzy! Faint! Light-headed! Nauseous! Recoiling, I vomited. Vomited again and again and again until I was gagging, spewing green bile. There was nothing left for my stomach to eject! I wanted to die. Die on the spot. Right there! Right then! I could not bear the agony that seized me! My entire body began to tremble, shivering uncontrollably! My bowels let loose! Spilled their contents, running loose down my legs! The stench rising to assail my nostrils, I was not even embarrassed. Did not care. Would no longer care for anything. I begged for relief! For death! I screamed to the deaf heavens. I no longer believed in God—would never believe in anything again. Yes, heaven was truly deaf – unmerciful as well—for a loving God would not have allowed this to happen.

I screeched violently, vociferously: "Oh vile, vile world! Cruel World! Ugly! Detestable! Gross villainy! Treachery! Evil incarnate! I do not wish to see this! It is unbearable."

My heart was in a fury. I was choking! Wailing. My head felt like it might burst! My body was gripped ferociously by spasms. I locked shut my eyes! My burning eyes! I wished to see no more! Only blindness would ease my shattered heart! I lost consciousness—this sight abominable—the shock beyond endurance – too much! Too, too much!

Then the sky opened up vociferously with an ear-splitting crack of thunder, drenching all in a torrential downpour, a drowning cascade of water blending the clay dirt with the oozing life-blood of the young freedom fighters, along with Jacques who lay prostrate in the sucking mud. Above this sickening miasma of puddles, scarlet life-blood running and blending with brown sienna-hued dirt, even the heavens were weeping.

Chapter 18

I did not know how long I slept—hours, days, months. I was oblivious to my surroundings. When I awakened for even a few seconds, I snapped my eyes tight shut again. Someone was ministering to me. Someone was putting cold compresses on my forehead. Someone was murmuring prayers day and night. Someone was spooning broth which dripped from my lips, drooling down my chin, and into the crevice of my neck. Someone. Someone. Someone. Not Papa. Not Mama. Not Jacques. They were **gone, Gone, GONE!** Never to be seen again. Who was this someone? I wanted to tell whomever I did not care to eat. Did not care to drink. Did not care to pray—for prayers had proven fruitless. Unheard. Unanswered. In vain. For naught. **I did not care to live, for life was meaningless.**

After a long comalike sleep—a torpor—I awakened to the sweet scent of gardenia. On a chair by my bedside, Grand-mere leaned over with a beatific smile

"Merci, Mon Dieu," she uttered thanks to God for this return of her precious grand-daughter.

This girl was all she had now, and she could not bear losing another. It would surely kill her. The nurturing of this child had been her salvation on that day weeks ago when she herself wanted to succumb to the oblivion of death. Jacques was gone, lined up with other teen saboteurs and shot en masse—executed. Their crime: slashing the tires of the German jeeps, filling their oil receptacles with paint; other mischievous pranks to antagonize the enemy—to retaliate in the only way helpless victims could. The scene was horrific. Rivulets of blood trickled from the limp and lifeless bodies of eight boys—mere teens—their lives cut short by this insanity. Jacques had been the last, at the end of the line, on the right. She recognized him immediately, although face-down on the muddy ground of the rectangular outdoor space— his shaggy mop of thick hair creating a halo round his head, fanning out in curling waves. Only a silent howl escaped her. Her voice was absent, unable to vocally confirm the unimaginable, grotesque scene spread out before her incredulous eyes. Her vision blurred; she attempted to focus; she wished for blindness so as not to confirm her utmost fear and sorrow. Unmoving, he lay prone in the dirt, lifeless. Time stood still. It stopped. She did not remember whether or not her legs carried her forward. Forward to what? To the corpse of her sweet boy! She had failed in her most sacred duty to protect him from harm. Or perhaps it was punishment for her most grievous sin. Her sin from eighteen years ago. The stubbornness lodged in her heart for all these years. A terrible waste of energy! And she steadfastly believed herself a Christian—sowing seeds of peace, love, charity, and hope. **HOPE!** There was no hope any longer. The future lay cruelly slaughtered before her. Something—someone fell against her leg—her granddaughter—Jeanne Marie—lay in a heap by her side—immobile—silent—lifeless too. But no—her pulse still beat—she was alive. **ALIVE!** This fact seemed to pierce the older woman's stagnant brain out of its reverie of shock and disbelief at what lay before her. She stooped over the girl, wrapping her arms around her, while others helped to carry her home to the house at the top of Rue Savoir.

PART V

THE AFTERMATH

CHAPTER 19

"**M**a belle petite-fille," Grand-mere's voice sounded hoarse with long, sleepless hours at the bedside. "You have been in a deep slumber." Relief was etched distinctly on her ashen face.

"Bonne-maman, **O-O-h-h-h**," Jeanne sobbed, her mind scalded with the horrific memory.

"Hush, my child." With gentle, caressing strokes she brushed back the light hair surrounding this beloved face. She could not lose this one who was now so vulnerable. She must be careful in her handling of this child or she might break. The older woman's words must be delicate, but their tone firm and certain; as if she knew for sure, "That this too shall pass." But of this she was no longer convinced. Nevertheless, she must, **must, must** insure that the youngster believes this—relying on the truth of the Biblical words. **TRUTH!** What truth remained here? **THEY— THESE WRETCHED BOSCH BASTARDS** had shattered the truth with their lies, **LIES, LIES, LIES! THEIR LIES AND DIS-TORTION OF THE TRUTH.** But she could not—dare not—here and now, in front of this fragile child—give vent to the deep pain and intense rage that threatened to make her heart stop forever. And if so, her granddaughter would have no one. **NO! SHE MUST ENDURE FOR THE SAKE OF THIS PRECIOUS GIRL. SHE MUST!**

Her rambling thoughts became scattered when Jeanne abruptly sat upright, pointing from the bed with her outstretched, trembling hand to some unknown place

"**RENÉ! RENÉ!**" she screamed. "**IN THE WALL! THE WALL!**"

"He's safe! He's safe away from here. Don't fret. He's safe."

"Me`me`, what is that chirping—so melodious, so beautiful. How is it possible it sings on these most woeful days?"

"Ma chere," replied Grand-mere, "I opened the windows to let in the cool fresh evening air. It is salubrious. Breathe deeply of its wholesomeness, as well as the scent from the lilac tree outside your window. That sweet melody you hear is from the nightingale who sings most sweetly on the darkest nights."

Yes, indeed, these had been the very blackest, most sorrowful, darkest of times.

CHAPTER 20

Gradually Jeanne Marie recovered—at least physically she gained her strength back. What she did not know was that during her illness, Farmer LaCloche's daughter Adele had been bringing provisions. Scanty as they were, Grand-mere was grateful that she and Jeanne were far from starving. In Paris they were eating pigeons and cats! Mon Dieu! Rations had been cut back to 140 grams of cheese and one egg per month. One egg, imagine! Adele LaCloche had been bringing half a dozen each week. In Paris there were hardly any meat, fish, milk, or butter. But the LaCloche girl had told Grand-mere that this would be her last trip. The family was barely able to provide for themselves. She did not need to add that Jacques was no longer there to help, and that the barter on which they had agreed—trading food in exchange for the lad's labor—was no longer. LaCloche himself was ailing, his rheumatism curbing his production. Though Jeanne did not see Adele, she overheard the conversation and felt that she could no longer be a burden. She must pull her weight now more than ever. If she took Jacques' place at the LaCloche farm, she could at least feed the pigs, collect the eggs, learn how to milk the cows.

So, on the following week, Jeanne made her first trek through the pine-scented woods to the farm. Picking her way carefully between the rocky ground, she heard a laugh—a sort of giggle—and taking cover behind a tree, Jeanne spied the same comely girl and young handsome German she had seen before. Frolicking, hands joined together, he was swinging the lass in a circle, her yellow dandelion plaited braid flying out behind her, silken wheat held together with string of brightly colored ribbon. As they twirled round and round in jocund play, their fresh, youthful faces turned upright—resplendent—toward the sky, Jeanne felt the pure joy that emanated from them. Their faces were glistening, gleaming under the dizzying speed of their near silent dance. Finally spent from the whirlwind of movement, they collapsed together on the mossy forest floor. And then as before, he leaned in to lovingly kiss her upturned face, rosy and slick with perspiration. His russet hair drooped heavy over his brow; the girl reached up and tamed it back, bringing her right hand slowly from the top of his head down the side of his face, and left it there resting against his cheek. Then lifting her left hand to his other cheek, she held his face between her gracefully tapered fingers. They remained connected by that mutual adoration. Reaching searchingly, he took the lass's hands, opened them reverentially, and planted kisses on both palms, nipping at first, then increasingly greedy, seeming as if her wanted to bite them, eat them, swallow them. Jeanne had never observed such ardor before and sensed that this was a marvelous and exquisitely beautiful expression of reciprocated affection. Although she felt ashamed of trespassing on a very private moment, she was mesmerized—could not pull herself away; for this was the purest form of romantic love she had ever witnessed. Jeanne thrilled with the vicarious experience of it. Suddenly, as before, the girl jumped up and ran toward the end of the woods which abutted the farm. Halting abruptly just before crossing into the wide expanse of shimmering purple lavender swaying in the breeze, she turned, stole a backward glimpse, and threw a kiss in his direction. When the splendid solider turned and trod in the opposite direction, Jeanne roused herself from this dream-like trance and followed in the girl's tracks. The same girl was milking the cow when Jeanne entered the barn.

"Bonjour. I am Jeanne Marie Molineau. I am here to offer my help to Adele and Monsieur LaCloche,"

"Oui, Oui," replied the girl. "My sister is inside and my father somewhere around."

"No need to stop your work," Jeanne replied. "I will find one of them"

Approaching the house, then curving her way around to the back, she came upon Monsieur fiddling with the cover of the cistern. Startled, he jumped when Jeanne spoke his name.

"So sorry, Monsieur. I did not mean to startle you, but the milkmaid directed me here to find you."

"No need to apologize, my dear. She is my other daughter Sophie. So very glad to see you well after … after …

"Yes," Jeanne saved him the discomfit. "We miss my brother terribly."

When LaCloche saw the girl's brimming eyes, he reached for her hand and said solicitously, with great emotion, "I am so sorry … so very sorry. They are evil, savage barbaric swine—the Bosch," his gravelly voice shook and his hand trembled. "That brother of yours—a good, brave lad, a fine boy with a good stout heart. Damn to hell every, stinking pig in the entire Hun army, the whole lot. **Damn them to hell! To hell,"** he bellowed as if in pain, shaking his head and stifling a sob.

After composing himself and wiping away his tears with a tattered handkerchief, he inquired, "What might I do for you."

"No. No. You misunderstand my purpose here. It is **what can I do for you?** I am better now and am aware that you are in need of help. Put me to work. I need to work outdoors in the sun. It will do me good. Please, let me help you and in this way, you will be helping me."

"As you wish, my child. I welcome your help and your company."

Within a short time, Jeanne was assisting Monsieur La-Cloche with more than farm chores. She became aware that in the dead of night he was assisting in the escape of downed British pilots. In addition, he was the leader of partisans receiving parachute drops of arms. He did not solicit her assistance, but she insisted forcefully to him and the other resistance fighters that a young, naïve-looking girl could be an asset in deflecting attention; and so at her own insistence, she too became part of the underground.

PART VI

A YOUNG GIRL GROWS UP

CHAPTER 21

Days passed. A month. Then timid knocking at the door—again in the middle of the night. Grand-mere instructed Jeanne to remain upstairs. She would see to the knocking, but Jeanne was no longer a child in need of such protection since she had seen **what no child should see**. There was labored breathing on the other side of the door.

"Madame, Madame. We come in peace to beg your mercy. Please, please, Madame, open up."

Silhouetted by the light of the moon, were two ragged, very dirty creatures, skeletal in shape.

They appeared distressed, distraught; one was shaking, the other was bloodied.

"What would you have of me?" asked Grand-mere. "Why did you come here?"

"For sustenance and cover," one beseeched. "We have managed to make it here from the city. All the members of our family were arrested, taken to the trains and transported to who knows where. They say..."

Grand-mere interrupted. "Yes, I've heard. But I have hiding space for just one, not two," she informed them. "And it can be only for a single night. You must be gone by morning."

They looked forlorn. "We cannot be separated," they said in unison. "We have no family but each other. Have mercy, please," they cried in unison.

Grand-mere looked at Jeanne—the first time ever she seemed to need her granddaughter's input.

"Grand-mere," the girl interceded. "I think I know a place for the second one."

"You know a place for the second one???" stammered her grandmother.

"Yes, let's feed them and then just before daybreak, I will take one somewhere safe."

"But where, Jeanne. No place is safe."

"Leave it to me; trust me," she replied with assurance. And for the first time, Grand-mere heard confidence in her tone.

After giving them some meager sustenance, they waited in the darkness until dawn approached. Jeanne led the way toward the forest while Grand-mere secreted the other visitor inside the wall.

Stealthily, Jeanne picked a path through the woods, keeping her charge close. She could not help but fondly remember the dazzling sweet scene with the loving couple she had observed in this copse. She now knew that the girl had been Adele's sister Sophie, the other daughter of Monsieur LaCloche. On this ebony-black night, ugliness, fear, and terror permeated these woods. At the edge, they hesitated, waiting, crouching for the right moment. Jeanne felt a great responsibility and told her charge to remain hidden until her return.

Farmer LaCloche was in the barn already busy with his work.

"I must speak with you," she said. "Now. Immediately. In the woods beyond is one who is in need of help. I believe you have a place for her,"

He looked at Jeanne cautiously. "Why do you think so?"

"Truly, monsieur, I am not sure. But if you can help, I will send her forward. If not, I must find a different place."

He seemed to understand what she was asking. "Yes, I can take her. Send her before it is too light. We must fight darkness with darkness."

CHAPTER 22

S ome weeks later, again there was commotion in the street—
bedlam—shouting—screaming—bellowing—voices   raised
in riotous shrieks: **"Whore! Fucking whore! Bitch! Collaborating bitch! Slut!"**

From the peepholes in the shutters, Grand-mere and
Jeanne could see it all. People were pushing, hitting, shoving, and
in the center of it all, being dragged through the jeering crowd,
was the pretty milk-maid from the forest and the farm. Jeanne
could see Sophie's tear-stained and horrified expression.

Those vile, ugly names reverberated again, again, again.
Others were taking up the chant when the colonel, emerged from
his office below, raised his pistol in a dramatic gesture, and shot
in the air. All sound ceased abruptly.

"Achtung! (Attention!) Stehen bleiben! (Halt; stay put!). *Ruhe!* (Silence)" he commanded. "Get a chair and place it here—here—in the center for all to see. Tie her to it! Tightly I say. Shame! Shame on you and all your sister collaborators. You filthy pig. You whore. You seduce and spoil our fine young German males with your sexy wiles. Your treachery leaves them soiled, contaminated!"

As ordered, they secured her upright in the wooden, straight-backed seat and the colonel spit at her feet.

"Mémè, what are they doing? She is guilty of nothing!" Jeanne lamented.

"What do you know about it?" queried Grand-mere.

"I saw them… in the woods. She and the German soldier. It was beautiful. Sublime. They danced and laughed and then he kissed her chastely—gently on the lips; that was all. She kissed him back and then went on her way. They did nothing dirty. She is no whore. It was pure and sweet and beautiful."

Jeanne began to weep, to shudder; for when she returned her gaze to the window, they had taken scissors – the keenly honed blades glinting in the sun and were cutting away her hair in huge clumps—her gorgeous silky tresses—pulling them taut—tugging roughly as she sobbed. Toward the rear of the crowd was the handsome young soldier, his mouth agape, his countenance tortured; but he remained frozen in shock on the cobblestones. He made no sound; he made no move. Like shafts of golden wheat, her hair lay strewn upon the ground, spattered with sunlight. Jeanne stood transfixed when around the corner stormed farmer LaCloche. He was screaming in a hoarse voice, his breathing ragged from exertion, his face ruddy, his stomp determined.

"What is it that you do?" he screeched at the top of his lungs. His chest was heaving up and down, up and down. All could see the veins bulging in his neck. His eyes were fiercesome wide. He struggled to contain himself, but in vain. He was trembling with rage, his shaking arms outstretched to his daughter secured uncomfortably to the chair, her arms twisted torturously behind her. Her head hung to her bosom and that too was rising spasmodically—up, down, up, gasping, down—short, staccato breaths alternating with her gulping sobs.

The colonel snarled, "*Steben bleiben!*" (HALT!) LaCloche approached his precious daughter, his heart breaking, straining painfully in his chest, choking off his air. All could see his terror, his grief, his sorrow, his intense love, his puzzled bewilderment.

"Steben bleiben!" repeated the colonel, but LaCloche seemed deaf and dazed as he lunged for his daughter. A shot rang out! A short, deafening blast!

Jeanne jumped in grand-mere's hold. Her breathing stopped. She gasped, transfixed in shock. First an anguished cry escaped; then she was keening, keening, keening.

"Oh, no-no-n-o-o-o-... not her... not again! Not again!"

Grand-mere was speechless, but she shook herself alert, opened wide her door, and braced herself for what was to come. With noble carriage and stoic dignity, she strode determined down the hill, her footsteps resounding on the cobblestone street. At the bottom, she bent forward to untie the knots, loosening the rope. Slumped heavily forward, eyes squeezed shut, Sophie was unwilling to take in the sight of her slain father just ahead of her. Coaxing the girl to stand, Grand-mere slipped Sophie's arm around her own shoulder, turned, and dragged the broken figure up the hill. Turning on the steps at the entrance of her house, she stood stark still.

"May God forgive you! *Quelle honte! Quelle honte!* **For shame! For shame!"** she shrieked at the top of her lungs. **"May God forgive you; you know not what you do."**

It took every ounce of strength to bear the girl's weight. Jeanne helped to lay the helpless, dazed Sophie upon the bed, to bathe her tear-streaked face, remove her clothing, and wrap the counterpane snugly around her shivering body. It was all they could do. And then they prayed as always.

CHAPTER 23

Jews escaping from the cities began to comb the countryside in a deluge; and with their arrival came more incredible *rumeur* about the heinous "final solution," by which the Nazis intended to eradicate the entire Jewish race. Grand-mere and Jeanne heard but could not believe, that upon arrival at some camps, Jewish mothers were forced to make a choice: if physically able, to present themselves for work as part of a *hilfsdienst* (volunteer unit) and abandon their small children; or to stay with their little ones and proceed to the gas chambers immediately. In one camp only two of six-hundred mothers presented themselves for work, while all others chose to die with their babes. More and more sought refuge behind Grand-mere's paneled walls. When Sophie had recovered under their tender ministrations, she seemed to have developed a new boldness. Her hair had begun to grow back in blond tufts sticking out every-which-way from her scalp. Stiff, short wisps poked out in pointed barbs here and there, but she did not seem to care. Grand-mere gave her a small but brightly colored print scarf of Provençal colors—red, bright yellow, ultramarine blue—and Sophie wrapped it round her shorn head and seemed to wear it proudly. Never again would she trust a German, and she would seek her revenge by working to defeat them.

When more than one came seeking over-night refuge at Rue Savoir, Jeanne now was the one to take control and ushered them through the woods to the farm. The cistern could hold a few more. All the better that the farm had fallen into disrepair, despite Adele and Sophie's efforts to keep the cows, chickens, and pigs producing. These refugees who escaped from the cities were much more severely malnourished than the villagers; and only through sheer will-power and the human desire to survive, did they make it to Provence. Many succumbed upon arrival. Death surrounded all. The LaCloche girls and Jeanne became what was known among the German Jews as *lagerschwestern,* referring to those women in the ghettos who bound together as sisters in their efforts to sustain their people.

One day as the German soldiers were performing their military exercises, marching ceremoniously through the village, their heavy hobnail boots stomping in unison on the cobblestones creating an intimidating bombardment of ear-splitting rhythmic cracks, a stranger standing beside Jeanne inquired, "A penny for your thoughts."

No longer caring about consequences, she replied adamantly, "Every single one should drop dead!"

Some days later, another stranger approached her, inquiring whether she would deliver a message for him.

"Deliver it yourself," Jeanne retorted.

"I wish I could," replied the stranger, "but I am under suspicion, so I will be followed; and, as a result, I will put others in peril."

The girl understood what he was saying and why she was needed. That began her clandestine work as an underground messenger. Each time she would be approached by someone different, and the address to which she delivered the note was never the same. Never—not once – did she open or examine the note she was carrying. In fact, Jeanne began to devise clever ways of hiding it from sight. One day, she had chosen to bake the crumbled note into a baguette which she wrapped in a colorful cotton dishcloth, then placed in her bicycle basket, along with mushrooms picked in the woods, some root vegetables, and a large bouquet of wild flowers. When suddenly ahead of her appeared a trio of soldiers on the same dusty path, her stomach clenched, her legs grew wobbly from anxiety, her mouth felt exceedingly dry—parched. Realizing that she could not hesitate, or all would be lost, she pumped her legs faster, faster, faster—quicker, quicker —gaining speed from an adrenalin rush. She felt her hammering heart would burst from the expenditure of all her energy to gain such momentum. There was a rhythmic throbbing in her temples. With reckless abandon, singing at the top of her lungs, she sped by. Her entire body was bathed in icy perspiration, trickling along her backbone and down her spine. Once past, she heard them laugh as one called her a "crazy girl—an *embecile*—with a few screws loose." But she was not deterred from carrying out the mission—to deliver the prized bread containing the secret message. Immediately after that, she learned of the demise of two local traitors—members of the Gestapo—despised for their collaboration with the enemy against their own villagers. Jeanne had an inkling that she had been the harbinger of the retribution they received for their despicable betrayal of their neighbors.

There were other missions on which she was not the courier of a message, but the deliverer of explosive material. On one close call, she emerged from the forest onto the sandy dirt path to suddenly encounter a burly, unshaven, middle-aged soldier idly smoking a cigarette. He was just a few feet before her, so close that Jeanne could see the stubble on his chin, smoke rising from his lips, exposing yellow, uneven rotting teeth. She was on foot, her bike beside her; for a split second, she considered hopping on, but then he addressed her.

"Bonjour, Mademoiselle," he greeted with a wry smile in heavily accented French. "Where do you go this fine day?"

Stiffening, Jeanne stopped short, groping mentally for a convincing response.

"Returning from an errand for my grand-pere," she replied cautiously, knowing it was a lie, and trying to steady the quaver in her voice.

"And what might that be?" he continued, gloating in his ability to startle and delay her.

From beneath the assorted articles in her basket, she retrieved two bottles of very fine local burgundy, its claret hue enhanced by the sun's sparkle upon it.

"Ah," he gurgled, "the very best! A rare treat!"

"Oui," she agreed, "and if you'll let me be on my way, I will make you a gift of one. As long as I don't arrive home totally empty-handed, I don't believe my grandfather will beat me."

"O-o-o-h, *my jeune fille*, I would not wish that either. Your offer is generous and very much appreciated," and with that Jeanne passed him a bottle and he dismissed her with a wave of his hand.

Oh! How very, very lucky to have escaped for the price of a bottle of wine. Covered beneath it were wires and other hard-to-get items needed for making explosive devices to detonate the train tracks. She had been delivering these for some time, but this was the nearest Jeanne had ever come to discovery. Danger and fear lurked everywhere.

Through her collaboration with the underground, Jeanne was also aware of the rough creation of a two-hundred-yard air strip, actually a path cleared through the fields for clandestine air drops of arms and soldiers. Two long vertical rows of lavender had been planted just over halfway down the runway, and at the end a patch of potatoes. This makeshift landing strip, code-named "Spitfire," was located some distance from the town on a hidden plateau. The lavender fields served as a camouflage for the moon-lit landings guided only by Resistance members holding torches. These covert operations were successful for some time until one black unfortunate night, an aircraft, larger than previous ones, proved too heavy to take off after landing, unable to lift off the short grassy runway. When the undercarriage snagged on the bushy stalks of lavender, it lost speed, necessitating the evacuation of all on board. It was a hellish event that halted all future activity since those caught were summarily executed. Jeanne was saved only by the fact that her grand-maman was ill that night with a temperature hovering around 102 plus degrees and she dared not leave her alone. Worse yet, as a reprisal, the relatives of the saboteurs were herded into the church, the doors barricaded and locked, and the church set ablaze. The inferno turned the sky blood orange with flames, as ferocious and searing as any concentration camp oven. Observers reported the agonizing shrieks that assailed the skies as the prisoners perished in the searing heat. Jeanne could only wonder if anyone had been hiding beneath the floor between the organ pipes during this ghastly conflagration. Unable to sleep for many nights, her nightmares scorched in her brain along with the ghoulish image of her precious brother Jacques in the center of it all, flaming tentacles snaking toward him from a fiery pit.

During the next year, Grand-mere seemed to be failing for the first time. Her hands shook violently; she appeared frail; arthritis plagued her so that she was frequently bent over in pain. Her once tall frame began to shrink, whether due to stress or age or disease, Jeanne could not tell; but it saddened and sobered her. Her bonne-maman had always been her guide, her strength, her mentor, her example. It had been some years since the loss of Jacques, and Jeanne was clueless as to the fate of her father and mother. **Grand-mere was ALL that she had left!!! I Needed** her. **Depended** on her. Would be left **bereft, untethered,** without her. If she lost her too, Jeanne did not want to live.

As if testing fate, the girl had become somewhat more reckless of late, almost wishing that the Germans would discover her underground activity hiding the escapees. Grand-mere, now weakened, did not protest or object. Jeanne had become the dominant one—the decision maker while the elderly woman was receding more and more into the background, sometimes sleeping many hours of the day. She had developed a persistent cough, which Jeanne sensed was a harbinger of worse things to come. In

her granddaughter's presence, she tried to stifle its nagging de-
mand to be released, but sometimes it insisted on being heard.

PART VII

A CONFESSION

CHAPTER 24

Her granddaughter—<u>GRANDDAUGHTER</u>. Could any word be sweeter? She repeated it again and again in her mind. BELOVED GRANDDAUGHTER! She could never have imagined all those years ago, that her son's marriage, which she had so strongly opposed, could possibly yield such sweet fruit in her old age. She had been adamant, vehement in her refusal to acknowledge the girl her son Francois had chosen and loved beyond reason. He was hopelessly smitten, she could see; but she **would not, could not** condone this relationship. And then he stopped seeking her approval. He just upped and married the girl and disappeared. **OH! How her heart ached. Her only child— cherished, treasured, doted on from infancy. No sacrifice had been too great to provide him with everything. They were very**

comfortable financially and so they gave him every advantage—she and her husband, long deceased. Oh! The longing for him—the yearning once he had made that irrevocable choice. Her son lost to her forever because of her stubbornness. Her heart had felt shattered—like sharpened shards of glass slicing it into tiny fragments. But still she did not seek them out—her son and his wife. His decision had been made, and she was too proud and hurt to reconcile. Oh, she had always been tenacious in her beliefs—her husband, more malleable than she, had often capitulated to her wishes because he loved her so, and respected that spine of steel that was, in some situations, a worthy attribute. She remembered the time when Francois had been a toddler with a raging fever. Rushing him to the hospital, they found it crowded, overwhelmed with sick people needing attention. They had been instructed to register at the admitting desk and sit until called. Her husband had begun to sign the list, but **she—she** had demanded that the child be tended to immediately.

They tried to pass her off. "Be seated, Madame, and wait your turn."

"Be seated?" she protested. "I will not wait to see my child suffer. He is seriously ill and needs a doctor. **NOW! NOW! NOW. The heat from his body is burning against my chest.**"

She was holding the limp Francois, the weight dragging at her; but still she maintained that perfect erectness that had caught her husband's attention and admiration the first time he saw her. Monsieur Molineau had known instantly that this was a woman of substance, of principle, and strength. He had initially been attracted to that very trait; but there were times during their years together that he found her to be unbending, obstinate in her refusal to accept what did not suit her high standards of human

106

behavior. Herself—she held to extremely high demands—set only by herself for herself—a sort of stalwart attempt to attain the highest pinnacle of virtue. She could be severe in her judgment of others—finding them wanting when they disappointed her. Her husband would attempt to point out that after all, people were merely human—with weaknesses, flaws, idiosyncrasies, and failings; but too often she would have none of it. It was as if she were aspiring to sainthood—canonization—and trying to bring everyone else with her. Monsieur Molineau wondered that his wife did not ever criticize him or accuse him of lacking in any way. Far from perfect, he was acutely aware of his own weaknesses—never significant—but still he was not a model of perfection. It was as if she loved him enough to overlook his shortcomings, and he knew she loved him deeply.

And in the next moment she had charged through the double doors, ignoring the protestations of the other patients seeking admission. Behind her, the doors closed and there was bedlam as others began pushing toward the entrance so that the gendarmes on guard had to intervene or it would quickly deteriorate into a mob scene. In an attempt to gain entrance and follow his wife, Monsieur Molineau received a quick thrust from a *gendarme's* bully club.

CHAPTER 25

One evening as Jeanne was helping Grand-mere into bed, she patted the elder's hand, pulling the counterpane around her bony shoulders.

"Sit. Sit. Please Jeanne Marie. We should talk" she said with a heavy sigh. The girl saw a seriousness in her eyes. Was it regret? Sadness? Jeanne couldn't quite read her.

"I must tell you something. It is long overdue. Difficult for me to tell and difficult for you to hear. First, I should tell you how very proud I am of the woman you've become. Courageous. Brave. I am aware of the work you and les *filles Cloche* have done to help these poor people escape their persecutors."

Jeanne wondered how Grand-mere was aware that Adele, Sophie, and she had devised means to provide the Jews with cover and safe haven. All three had become part of a clandestine group hiding Parisian Jewish children in the countryside. A well in the herb garden of a nearby estate became the depository for the secret lists of children needing safe placement. A water-tight container was rigged to a thin wire and into this, a fellow underground conspirator would place identity cards, with description of child or children who would soon arrive. Inside would also be ration cards and money for their maintenance, as well as for pay-offs if necessary. The money was rumored to be provided by a wealthy woman Suzanne Spaak, code name "Suzette" — known as *sauveteur d'enfants Juifs,* who was said to have helped over one thousand children escape capture. Some Jewish furriers in Paris also contributed to the mission. Some of the older children had been taught to recite the Catechism and were coached with cover stories as to how they had come to a certain family in Provence — for example, as relatives displaced by the bombing in the cities and evacuated by parents to extended family in the countryside. These unfortunate waifs — some as young as five-years-old, one still sucking a calloused thumb — gaped beseechingly at the saviors with wide and imploring eyes. Most had been evacuated from bleak, packed wards in state-run children's homes and fortress-like orphanages, their destination after parents had been arrested and deported to Auschwitz and Ravensbruck. Jeanne and her co-conspirators had been told of three convoys that left Drancy for the first camp on February 9, 11, and 13, carrying 460 children, most of whom were gassed upon arrival. Those who were brought to the countryside were homeless, friendless, parentless, filthy, skeletal, pale, malnourished, often clinging to the hand of an older child, dragged along stumbling, often half-asleep. Some would immediately fall into the girls' arms, oblivious to all but the longed-for comfort of a loving embrace, held tightly against a breast. It was chilling to realize that, if not for Jeanne, her friends, and other collaborators, they would have joined their unfortunate brothers lined up en masse for the incinerators in the death camps. Their job was to have prearranged placement for the children among willing farmers or townsfolk. All was very risky. Relying on trusted contacts, the women had a terrifying mission, never certain of who was trustworthy. Acutely aware that execution was the penalty for hiding Jews, the girls did not care if they could save even just one life, and they rescued many. From Paris, they managed to obtain copies of the revolutionary paper *J'Accuse*. The latest issue alerted that "two thousand Jewish children—aged 2 to 12—had just been sent to an unknown destination in the East. Endless trams with sealed cars had delivered them to torture and death. The heart-rending cries of innocent victims, drowning out the sound of the wheels, sowed terror and horror all along the road. The news article asked, "Mothers, is there anything in the world, more inhumane, more barbaric than being ripped away from parents with animal savagery... These horrors happened here, in our sweet land of France, with the complicity of the French government, collaborating with those who starve us, plunder our wealth, hold our people captive, and murder the patriots fighting for a free and happy France... Do not by your silence become accomplices... *Il faut faire quelque chose.*" ("*Something must be done*"). Jeanne, along with the LaCloche sisters, knew that the fate of these small prisoners rested in their hands, and **they did what had to be done.**

Adele had managed to obtain some tight black netting which she lined with black tarp. It was her clever idea to secure it tightly to the bottom of the rusted tractor idly sitting in the barn.

If tied securely just so, it would hold the weight of a small, thin person slung beneath. In their farmhouse, they had also hidden individuals in the wall behind a large wooden break-front that had belonged to Madame LaCloche. Very weighty to move, it covered a small opening in the wall into which escapees could hide. If the place were torn apart, it would easily be found; but so far no one had come searching. They could allow their small charges to stay a night or two, but then they had to keep moving. With the selfless aid of guides and of other saboteurs, some were conveyed to Switzerland, Spain, Portugal. Provence was only one stop on a very perilous journey. Jeanne and the LaCloche girls continued to make use of the cistern so they were busy day and night.

"My dear, dear child," began Grand-mere, "You have brought me so much joy I did not deserve. I am not worthy to have you, but I have thanked God every single day of my life for you and your brother. I did not deserve such precious gifts," she repeated sadly.

"Mémè, whatever are you saying? You have given us everything—everything. We were fortunate to be sent to you."

"Oh, child, ma chere, if you only knew you would hate me and damn me to hell."

"Grand-mere, you are not making sense."

"Oh, yes, I am. If you only knew my sin—my most grievous sin, for which I have paid dearly. They say God forgives every transgression, but mine he did not. I have paid the ultimate price."

Grand-mere's hands were trembling. This conversation was taking its toll.

"I must make a confession now, before it is too late. It may be too late already. But **please, please do not hate me. I was a**

foolish, adamant woman. Your grand-pere warned me often about my unbending nature."

Jeanne wondered about this rambling. Perhaps Grand-mere was hallucinating, out of her mind. It sounded like a death-bed confession. So tightly was Grand-mere clutching Jeanne's hands, that the white knuckles bulged through her blue-veined, almost translucent skin. Jeanne's initial impulse was to flee. She did not want to hear what Grand-mere might say.

"Ma chere Jeanne," she struggled with what was to come. "Many years ago, my beautiful fine son, your father Francois, fell in love with a girl. As all young people in love, he was ecstatic. It was easy to know his feelings because his face was radiant when he spoke of her—Cecille, Cecille, Cecille. Of course, your grand-pere and I were happy for him to have found this love. He talked of her constantly. He was 'walking on air' as they say of those in the throes of love."

"When are we going to meet this prize?" asked grand-pere one evening.

"Soon, soon," replied your father Francois.

"But soon was long in coming. First, there was the excuse that her mother was ill. Then she had to take her university exams. Then there was a blizzard that closed down the entire city for days. In my heart I knew something was not right. Perhaps she was with child and embarrassed to meet us? So, one evening I sat Francois down."

"You know we love you and want to see you happy, but I sense you are delaying our meeting with the girl you've chosen, and I would like to know the reason for the hesitation to introduce us."

"He looked uneasy, his eyes cast downward. He had **never** been uncomfortable with me. Why, he would come thundering through the door, sweep me off my feet when I was at the stove cooking, and twirl me round and round. Then dip the ladle in the pot to taste"

"'H-m-m-m! So good. Delicious. You are the best—the best—the best—in every way!'"

He was always like that with me. When he was a schoolboy, if I wore a pretty dress, he'd say in an adoring voice that I looked '*magnifique*'—would reach up and fiercely hug me good bye in front of all his classmates and never felt embarrassed. He was happy all the time. Exuberant! Full of life. Life. Life. Life."

A tear trickled from the corner of her eye. She was breathing hard, struggling for air. Her chest rose and fell in a type of ragged rhythm. Her vise-like grip on Jeanne's hands confirmed her fear that the girl might run before she managed to release her burden.

"Ah, Jeanne, I was so wrong. So wrong. So stubborn. Unbending. So very foolish. What a terrible waste of energy. I have been trying to atone all these years. And still there is no respite. No relief. The regret—the pain is always there no matter what I do to expiate my sin—my most unforgiveable transgression."

Her granddaughter tried to console with soothing words, stroking her lined face.

She whispered, "There, There, Bonne-maman. You always told me nothing was ever unforgiveable. Nothing was ever the end of the world. That after the darkest winter, spring would surely come again. And I have always trusted your words. These words now contradict all that you have taught me—that **NOTHING... NOTHING... is ever unforgiveable.**"

"Ah, Jeanne, how do you know that? You are the innocent victim of my long-held deceit. My secret error. But I also did it for you. Forgive me, but I did it for you and Jacques to protect you. To protect you."

The girl believed her grand-mother was senselessly rambling—incoherent—until the old woman whispered as if confessing a secret no-one should hear.

"Your mother Cecille was a Jewess. A Jew. That is the part your father could not tell us. Why, we were Christians!" With that she gave a bitter laugh. "Christians. And was it Christian for me to reject her—this innocent Jewish girl whose only sin was to love my beautiful boy? **I, OF ALL PEOPLE, SHOULD KNOW WHY SHE LOVED HIM SO. I LOVED HIM TOO—BEYOND ALL MEASURE.**" She laughed again sardonically. "And so, I lost them both. A loss so great... so great... until she—Cecille—Cecille— why did I never say her name—so many wasted years—her name Cecille—she who gave me my greatest gift. A gift I did not deserve. I did not deserve you. She sent me her children. To save you. She loved you so. She didn't care about herself. Only that you be saved. She even sent Baptism certificates. She had you baptized in the Church. They are not forged certificates. They are real. She could do nothing for her beloved Francois, but she did all for you. She took an arduous job in a factory to send money for your care. Why! she had a university degree, but Jews were forbidden to work in any capacity. She was denied professional employment. When she entrusted you to my care, she knew she was in danger of being transported. There was no escape for her. If she considered relocating, fleeing, where would Francois find her when he returned. Francois. Francois. He never returned."

Absorbing all this in silence, a shocked Jeanne did not stir. After a long while, the girl leaned in to kiss her beloved grand-mere, who, exhausted with this purging of her conscience, was lying there in death-like stillness. Jeanne pulled the quilt snug around her shriveled body, then turned and descended the stairs.

In the kitchen, the young girl sat at the antique table—so familiar—dented and marred with years of use. Shuddering, Jeanne began to cry—not for herself—her losses—her father, mother, brother Jacques—but for her beloved grand-mere—for the pain she harbored silently all these long years, for the onerous burden of guilt she bore so heavily that weighed upon her heart, for her foolishness in believing her obstinacy was unforgivable. Unforgivable? The only failure in a life of goodness, generosity, and unconditional love. Why had her grandmother been so hard on herself? Why could she not forgive **HERSELF?** Jeanne certainly could—she who owed her everything—her very life. And her mother Cecille. How brave! How loving! How devoted a mother! Willing to sacrifice herself, but **NEVER** her children. Yes, Grand-mere had made an error in judgment, but she had been making up for it all these years in her efforts to hide, protect, and save these Jews, perhaps motivated by the grievous rejection of her son's beloved Cecille.

CHAPTER 26

Beyond endless fields of sunflowers, Grand-mere was buried in the village graveyard beside her beloved husband. Now Jeanne was truly alone on this earth, but she was unable to shed tears. It was as if the events of the last few months had turned her to stone. Although the sun was shining peach-gold, the spring flowers bobbing their spritely heads in the soft breeze, Jeanne felt numb and was glad for it—this complete loss of feeling. Perhaps it was her psyche's defense mechanism to protect her from the anguish of any more assaults on her emotions. It wasn't just the loss of Grand-mere, her greatest support and source of stability throughout this crazily tumultuous, unstable, unfathomable apocalypse; but any sense of sanity and humanity was becoming dimmer and dimmer every day. Two days before Grand-mere's death, as Jeanne was rounding the corner of nearby Rue Chantel, she saw a fellow—a father—being hauled by Gestapo, dragged from his front-door onto the pebbled pavement. Wielding a cudgel, a German officer was shouting, screaming obscenities, demanding the man tell them where he had obtained the black-market food. His eyes were tightly closed so as not to see the blows they reined upon him, one, then another, then another. His emaciated wife was hysterical, a screaming infant upon her shoulder, a toddler hiding his face in the folds of her ragged, much-mended skirt. Upon hearing the commotion, villagers had assembled and stood helpless, frozen in dread. The victim was now on his knees, blood pouring profusely from the side of his ear, his right eye totally closed but still dripping globs of thick scarlet fluid that coagulated into purple stains before him. Some of the bystanders were weeping, one old woman collapsed, praying, "Mon Dieu, Mon Dieu..." Ironically, the smallest, weakest man in the crowd tried to push forward cursing audibly, but three others—much stronger—held the would-be-rescuer back as he struggled wildly against their restraint. The father was on the ground now, writhing in agony from the multitude of kicks, those abhorrent glossy boots gleaming eerily from the sun reflected in the lethal pointed toes. Two of the Germans roughly pulled him to his feet as the commanding office grabbed the infant from its mother's grip and thrust it roughly, still swaddled in its thin, dull graying blanket, beneath the wheels of the jeep, its olive-green background adorned with those abhorrent, omnipresent swastikas. The wife wailed, her horrifying shrieks rending the sky above, teeming with puffy, white-blossom clouds. How could Heaven and its angels look down upon this vile atrocity? How could the cerulean Provençal sky, the background canvas for so many artistic

118

masterpieces that captured its ethereal beauty, look down so bril-liantly on this nightmarish scene of darkest evil. Instead, the sheer desecration upon this gorgeous landscape should have cast about it such a pall of blackness as to obliterate the brightness of that fiery orb lending witness to it all.

"**See what we do to criminals who dare to disobey our regulations?!? See, all of you who cry and stare and weep and resist. We are** *il vainqueur* **(the conqueror), and we will bide no interference. Do not try to thwart our occupation of this place. The sooner you submit, the better you will find yourselves. See the consequences of efforts to defy our rules!!!**"

At that, the officer swung himself adroitly behind the wheel of the jeep, the hideous vehicle transformed into a death machine. Putting it in gear with a horrible, ghastly grinding screech, he mercilessly drove over the babe, crushing its bird-like, delicate bones, crunched and splintered beneath the vehi-cle's ponderous weight. Mewling sorrowfully, the household cat lapped at the tiny remains. A hushed silence prevailed. Not one sound—no weeping, no sobbing, no gasping, no protestation—muted in stone-like horror. The mother fainted; the father lay still, as stricken dead. The witnesses, as if in dazed shock, dispersed in various directions. Some had to be led and supported away or they might drop. Jeanne felt disgust, nausea, heaviness of heart, despair, but relief that Grand-mere had been too ill to observe this *sacrilege*. Surely it would have been the final blow. But something died that day in all who witnessed in frozen incredulity this mad-ness that defied description. The trauma had been so branded in their collective consciousness that no one dared to speak of it, even to each other. It was as if their tongues were tied in eternal muteness. Upon returning home, those who had seen, remained speechless, walking as if in a trance, unable to give voice to those who questioned the witnesses on what had happened. Some went immediately to bed, closing the shades against that damnable sun that dared continue to cast its brightness upon such a day of infamy. Others went directly for the bottle, draining it in greedy gulps, impatiently hoping for the stupor, the torpor that would assuage the searing memory of what they'd seen. As for Jeanne, neither sleep nor alcohol would ever obliterate this atrocious memory. So, it was no wonder that at Grand-mere's burial a few days later, her granddaughter was totally devoid at last of all feeling—a walking zombie.

PART VIIII

THE GERMAN DEFEAT

Chapter 27

1945

The detested invaders had withdrawn, but not before the townspeople blew up the bridge spanning the river to delay their ignominious retreat. Word had reached those in the countryside that the Allies had liberated Paris and were progressing west. There was talk of the Americans finding death camps, atrocities, the scope of which was unimaginable. For Jeanne all existed in a blur, as if shell-shocked. She had never quite recovered from the week grand-mere died following the mind-shattering annihilation of the babe. Insensate, she continued to live but not to really live—to merely exist. Sophie had somehow fared somewhat better than Jeanne. Her hair had grown thicker and more luxurious than before—its blond highlights so glossy as it cascaded in waves around her face. But Jeanne had lost all her spirit. Though both LaCloche sisters visited, bringing nourishment, she rarely talked, and then in hesitant whispers. They found her listless and lethargic, and painfully thin. She could sit still, motionless for hours, the house unswept, untended, the windows dull and dusty. All curtains were drawn tight; she did **not** want to see outside. All was darkness perhaps reflecting her deep depression. She was broken—had lost all interest in living. The days dragged on in uneventful hours of idleness—emptiness—barrenness. **Nothing, Nothing. They had destroyed all and left NOTH-ING.**

Occasionally Adele would lead Jeanne outdoors, but she only craved the oblivion of sleep. The delight she used to take in the waving fields of fragrant lavender—marveling at the beauty of the hues—the gradations of purple to violet to lilac—she did not even notice now. And the warming sun she used to relish upon her neck and arms—to bask and luxuriate in its comforting warmth—now felt icy cold—bitter cold—no heat could permeate her body—her skin—her wounded soul. Adele and Sophie worried for her. **NOTHING**—nothing—could rouse her from this deadened state—this overwhelming moroseness. **She felt empty. Void. Lifeless. NOTHING.**

CHAPTER 28

SIX MONTHS LATER

Jeanne did recover enough to do some household chores, but her heart remained heavy and her mood morose. One day, while hanging wet laundry on a clothesline, she spied someone approaching from the distance. The stance of the figure seemed familiar—a sort of loping gait; but the bright lemon sun shone so blindingly as to obliterate her vision. As he came closer across the wide expanse of meadow—more distinctly into view— she gasped in recognition and dropped the clothespins. Unkempt, wild-haired, and more mature, he still was recognizable, and she ran towards him. Lifting his arms to clutch her tightly to him in an all-encompassing embrace, he leaned his head into her shoulder and began to sob—big heaving sobs; for it was the first time in what seemed an eternity that he held someone dear to him. She let him cry for what seemed an interminable time, and when he lifted his head, his tear-filled eyes looked deeply into hers.

"Jeanne, Jeanne Marie, …" he repeated the name as if savoring its sweet sound on his lips.

Later, he told her how often in these past years he had whispered that name in his fitful, restless sleep, in his tortured dreams! Perhaps, he thought, this too was a dream—but the heft of her body seemed real with warmth that permeated not only his fatigued body, but also his wearied soul.

"Jeanne, Jeanne Marie," he kept mouthing over and over, as a sort of mantra. Indeed, it had been a saving mantra for a long time, like a prayer that inspired hope in the never-ending miasma of his tortured experiences. It was as if he had used up all his energy to reach her; for he seemed to falter, swaying with the girl upon the dewy, emerald grass, yellow daffodils vibrant against the white sheets billowing in the gentle breeze, creating an immaculate canopy above the pair, a perfect scene for an artist's palette.

Silent. Mute. They grasped each other tightly, as if for dear-life. René released her first, staring Jeanne full in the face. Although he appeared unscathed, unscarred, his eyes betrayed a haunted, terrified glaze. Tentatively, he reached up with a calloused thumb to reverently trace the outline of her face as if in awe. **THIS, this** is what he had survived for… for this moment to see her once again. **THIS IMAGE. THIS VISAGE, so precious to him, had kept him going, had given him power to rise each time he fell.** He'd clawed for it each time he felt he could not rise again, his knees buckling beneath him. It had egged him on through fatigue, sickness, fevers, miles and miles of fleeing from the dogs, his omnipresent pursuers no matter where he went. In his heart and mind, her image was always with him. It was this vision that had saved him, the one shred of hope that he would survive to see her again. He **DID NOT** need to speak, to voice his joy; for she could read it in his face and feel it in his grasp.

After a while of holding each other as if for dear life, they rose, and she led him to the house. Guiding him to the sofa, she fetched a basin, heated some water scented with lilac soap, and returned to remove his tattered boots, slowly releasing the laces as if they were the booties of a sleeping babe. He required a softness of touch, she could tell, because he seemed fragile, vulnerable. Unbuttoning his filthy jacket and sweat-stained shirt, she loosened its collar and began to bathe his face, his neck with caressing strokes. He seemed unaware as if in a coma-induced heavy slumber, the only sound his rhythmic soft snores, occasionally interspersed by a contented sigh. After some time, she left him there and went into the kitchen to prepare some health-some brew. Upon awakening sometime in the late afternoon, he seemed disoriented—not sure of his whereabouts; but when he saw her standing above him, he smiled at last—somewhat shyly—not remembering their earlier embraces outdoors. Rising to take the hand which she willingly extended, he followed Jeanne into the kitchen where she had laid out an immaculate, crisp white linen cloth and pretty china painted with the delicate wildflowers abundant in the countryside. He had not eaten at such a table since he had left the village. Still it seemed a fantasy too precious to be real, so he did not speak for fear that sound would wake him from this awesome delusion. But, her hand in his, her flesh, so soft, was real. They ate in silence, relishing each sip, each bite. Neither spoke a word. Later she led him outdoors where, as the setting sun cast orange and magenta slashes against the Provençal sky, they sat side by side in hefty wooden, white arm-chairs, her hand in his. It was the first time in many months, Jeanne felt the restorative heat of the setting sun soaking through her.

After what seemed an eternity, René spoke first. "You can't imagine how I've lived for just this moment—to return home—to you. If I had not found you here, I could not go on."

"My sweet René, I am the only one left. My mother, my father—I have not seen them in more than four years. Jacques was killed, you know, and Grand-mere is gone too. Your family also—your parents and sister Monique never returned."

"I know," he replied with resignation. "I've already checked there, and everything has changed. Someone else is living in the house,"

And so, they talked for hours, sharing their pain, their losses, their experiences—all past now—but not forgotten—never forgotten.

The next day, with no home to which René could return, the pair rambled through the woods to the LaCloche farm. All remained still, nothing operational. Adele and Sophie welcomed René with open arms, like a long-lost relative returned at last. René felt maybe he could get the farm going again—which they agreed was worth a try. Each night he returned to Grand-mere's ochre house on the hill from which so many ugly, vile, evil events had been witnessed. The couple lived together there for many months before being united in holy marriage. It was only much later that Jeanne learned the sweet and gentle René, that same boy who used to create rhyming poems for her, had become the famous and highly respected French poet René Char, the defiant resistance leader—code-named Alexandre—instrumental in the liberation of France.

CHAPTER 29

Another from the past arrived some months later, emerging from the edge of the woods while René was out plowing the LaCloche fields. For a long while, he hung back, covered by the dense foliage, just waiting, hovering, hesitant. But then he saw her—the pale-skinned milkmaid—still ethereally beautiful, but somehow changed. How could she not be changed after all that she'd endured? Their acquaintance had cost her dearly—the shorn tresses the least of her losses. But for him, she might still have her devoted father who had sacrificed his life for her.

"How dare he intrude upon her now?" he questioned himself.

Yes, he too had lost all—his soul, his country, his purpose, his sense, his moral code—he **had** once been a decent, upright young man trying to find his place in the world. But just at that age when he should have been starting his education toward an honorable career, he had been conscripted into the army of The Third Reich by the Fuhrer—the Fuhrer, that **madman—insane with power and greed**—the architect of so much tragedy and devastation with his despotic desire for world power. How could this German youth have been so misled, so misguided, so very, very, wrong?!? So many other unfortunate lads had been procured to carry out the heinous orders of the Reich. At the time Johann felt he had no choice. But there are always choices. If he had chosen to refuse, he might be dead now; but there were times throughout the war when he'd consider death preferable, particularly in the situation with Sophie LaCloche. He had been stricken with horror when he saw her forcibly taken, ruthlessly bound, and mercilessly shorn of all those luxurious, honey-blond tresses which had first attracted him to her. Had been doubly shocked at the tragic fate of her father. Had stood frozen to the spot throughout it all. Oh, what a shrinking, detestable coward he had proved himself to be. Aghast, he had just stood by, a paralyzed observer of the wretched, chilling scene as it unfolded before his stricken eyes. Had he intervened, surely, he too would have been shot, or at the very least transported to an *arbeitslager* (labor camp) and issued a *haftlingnummer* (prisoner number). The guilt, regret, and shame hung so heavily around his person, that living had become so onerous a burden he wished himself dead at times. But no matter how much he deliberately put himself in harm's way to achieve his own demise, he was always spared, discovering that somehow, he was still miraculously alive. It was almost as if WHO-EVER determined such things—God, he supposed, if there were a God—had deemed that a life of hell on earth was more just punishment for him. Johann felt that an entire life of atonement would not suffice to make up to this blameless maiden the harm, the shame that he had caused her. Surely, he must LOVE her—if after all this time, he still carried her image with him everywhere. Could not forget those hours of absolute bliss spent with her in the sylvan woods. It was not mere lust, for they had never indulged in any intimacy. To him then she seemed an angel—too sweet, too pure—a transcendent being who had transported him to a type of spiritual level not to be sullied with physical passion. How had the purest relationship he'd ever experienced turned into such blackness. And now, whatever was he doing here? What could he possibly expect from her after the defilement of her reputation, her public humiliation, his failure to respond in any way, his cowardly and traitorous abandonment. All he knew was that he had been unable to forget her; and with their encounters in the woods, he experienced a spiritual transcendence to a plane of sheer bliss never before known.

And abruptly coming out of his reverie, he ventured forward from the cover of copse and inched forward, slow step by slow step. He could not run even if he wanted too, crippled as he was with just one leg. He was halfway across the open expanse, when she shaded her eyes against the glare of that omnipresent Provençal sun and saw him silhouetted beneath it. In disbelief, in shock, she stared as he lumbered unsteadily toward her. It seemed forever for him to reach her; and to his utter amazement, Sophie lifted her hand against the dazzling sun to shade his eyes so that she might peer more closely into them. His heart thrumming in his chest, Johann dared not speak; he was breathless from the effort it took leaning on the crutch to cross the wide, grassy field. She saw the pain and regret, the desire for forgiveness in addition to his physical impairment; and with that, she saw all she needed to see. Taking his free hand, she led him toward the farmhouse.

CHAPTER 30

12 MONTHS LATER

The war had been over for some time. Some aspects of normalcy resumed. Both René and Johann joined their efforts to resume the production of the farm. But anger, distrust, and resentment were the remnants of a bitter war. Villagers continued to shun both Sophie and the German Johann so that it was necessary for them to relocate in Germany. René thrived on the work outdoors surrounded by the beauties of this provincial setting. While hiding, wandering all those years in exile, he had yearned for this peace, tranquility, and contentment. Finally, home at last, he intended never to leave again. More significant was that Jeanne Marie was expecting their first child which was a harbinger of happier days. They had survived to usher in a new generation. **LIFE! LIFE! A NEW BEGINNING,** after so much death and carnage. Jeanne Marie recalled Grand-mere's wise words from *Ecclesiastes:* "For everything there is a season. A time for every purpose under heaven. A time to be born and a time to die. A time to weep, and a time to laugh. A time to mourn, and a time to dance." Oh, if only Grand-mere could see the wooden cradle René had recovered from the attic and polished to a glorious sheen. The immaculate, crisp white dotted-Swiss skirt Jeanne had sewn for it. The fresh ruffled curtains embellishing the windows in the nursery, which had once been Jacques' room. Oh, how her heart ached for him—for her mother and father as well, but that yearning was now offset by an anticipation, an eagerness she had never known before. She felt **ALIVE** again, invigorated with the babe she carried within her; and she roamed freely outdoors with a hope that had so long been repressed. The once tightly shuttered windows of the ochre house at the top of Rue Savoir were thrown open wide once again; and the fragrant scents from the shimmering meadows of myriad flowers wafted inside to aerate the sunny rooms. Both she and René, who had shyly loved her even as a young girl, could not have been more exultant. They hoped their time "to weep… and mourn" was over; and that their "time to laugh… and dance" was at hand. And then suddenly one day, a visitor wended his way up the cobbled street to the front door of the house at the top of the hill. He tapped gently and then entered when no one answered. Curiously and silently, he roamed around downstairs, peeking into the rooms as if taking everything in. He was encouraged to see two rinsed cups drying on the drainboard of the sink. From every window, he savored the wondrous natural beauty of rural Provence. Finally, he ascended the stairs to find a young woman placing a small mattress snugly in a hand-carved, antique wooden cradle. He gasped as he took in this preparation for a new arrival and gasped again when the pregnant mother-to-be turned to face him. Was this possible? Could this striking, self-possessed young woman be his beloved daughter he'd last seen as a budding pre-teen.

They stared intensely at each other, both too shocked to speak.

"Papa!" she uttered in a high-pitched voice.

At the same time, he spoke her name "Jeanne Marie" in the tenderest of voices.

They embraced tightly and over her shoulder, he took in the contents of the room.

"What is **THIS?**" He gaped, taking in her rounded form.

"Oh, Papa, Papa. How can I possibly tell you all there is to tell!?! You are alive! You are back! You are home! Mon Dieu! I had given up hope! So long! It has been so long!!

"Oui, my beloved daughter," he replied sadly. "So very, very long. So much sadness. So much suffering."

They cried for a long time in each other's arms, both wondering how they could possibly tell all that had transpired in the years of their separation. But, finally they heard the back-door slam below, and Jeanne took her precious father's hand to descend the stairs. René appeared puzzled since he had never met her father Francois, and Jeanne proudly introduced her husband to her father. All three seemed overwhelmed at first by this surprise; but soon Francois was seated in Grand-mere's armchair only to learn of his mother's passing. Of course, he was greatly saddened, but the most unbearable news was the agonizing loss of his precious boy—Jacques. At that, he seemed to cringe in pain, actually pressing the palm of his hand tight against his chest as if he felt his heart were about to explode, to burst. He doubled over. He had no words. He paled, his face a contorted grimace. Tears of grief, for so long unshed, ran unchecked down his creased and weather-beaten face. He mumbled incoherent words. Only the name "Jacques... Jacques" could be deciphered. Jeanne and René escorted him to a room upstairs, undressed him, and put him to bed. Then they held each other tightly all through that night, as if to never, ever let each other go again. It is said that nothing good ever comes from war; but after years of agonizing losses and relentless suffering, these three survived, reunited to face the world together once again, finding comfort, solace, strength, and renewed life, nourished and sustained by the salubrious warmth of the omnipresent, radiant Provençal sun.

AFTERWORD

This book is dedicated to treasured friend **Rosa Cotton** who inspired me to write about these events. As a young girl growing up in Belgium during WWII, she personally witnessed the invasion and occupation by the Germans. Their presence in her town cast a pall that affected the peaceful lives of her family and neighbors which she has remembered all her life. At 14, she became a messenger for the underground, then known as the White Brigade. Some of the experiences of this book's main character, Jeanne Marie, are taken from **Rosa's** life. Not only did my mentor share her experiences with me, but also the raw feelings engendered by the Nazi occupation. **Hers** was one of the houses they requisitioned for boarding a German soldier. In this novel, **she** is Jeanne Marie when on a mission, she flies past the enemy soldiers on her bicycle carrying a secret message. **Rosa** also witnessed the book's shocking scene in which the baby was forcibly taken from its mother's grasp. Moreover, **her father** is the basis for farmer LaCloche, a character in this book, who builds a clever hiding place for Jews. **Rosa** is Jeanne Marie when she refuses to read the German textbooks provided the school students. **She** is the girl approached by the stranger who asks her to deliver a secret message. So, in many respects this is **her** story, although her experiences were shared by many Europeans at that sad time in history. Although for most of Rosa's lifetime, she refrained from discussing any of the past; at age 90, she has contributed her memories to this novel. When long ago, I realized that Rosa had a story to tell, she told me that it was "too sad a story;" that she had seen "what no child should see"; hence, the title I took from her own words.

Actually, I was first inspired to write such a story follow-ing a trip to Provence four years ago. While on a river cruise along the Rhone, we stopped at picturesque and charming villages be-tween Lyon and Arles, including Beaune, Avignon, and others in between. I was captivated by their natural beauty and old archi-tecture, as well as their history. In one village, the local guide who had been born and raised there after the war, told us of one day that she was walking home from school to the top of the street where she lived with her grandmother and parents. As it was raining hard, she took cover under the awning of a café/bar at the bottom of the hill to escape the downpour. An ancient man was sloshing through the puddles and looked over in her direction. "Why are you standing **there**?" he bellowed at her accusingly.

"To get out of the rain," she shyly responded.

"Go home, little girl, and ask your parents why **no one should ever go near that place!**"

When indeed she inquired of her family what the elderly villager had meant, they told her how the cafe had been requisi-tioned as the commandant's headquarters during the German oc-cupation. She also brought us to her grandmother's house at the top of the hill and encouraged us to look very closely at the shut-ters, now old and peeling. None of us could discern the tiny, mi-croscopic holes her grandmother had instructed the handy-man to drill in them. In fact, her grandmother had indeed hidden fleeing Jews within its walls and was able to see from behind the closed shutters all that went on at the café-turned-headquarters at the bottom of the street. In my story, you will recognize this as Rue

Savoir where much of the action in this book takes place. The local guide also took us to the square where the village boys were executed for their chicanery intended to damage and dismantle German jeeps, etc. So much of *What No Child Should See* is based on actual events and people.

Many years ago, when I first met Rosa, she was extremely reticent and mentioned very little of her life in Europe before emigrating to the US. But as we developed a close relationship, she opened up about her past. I was a hungry listener since I am very interested in history, particularly WWII and Hitler's rise to power. It has never ceased to amaze—actually astound me—that one ambitious, demented individual—the embodiment of evil—consumed with the megalomaniac desire for power—could unsettle the world order as he did and set in motion tragedy and devastation on such a gargantuan scale. I am indeed grateful that Rosa finally decided to share her memories of this historic period with me.

Appendix

As I researched more and more about this period in history, I was appalled at the lack of interference by many to thwart Hitler's plan to annihilate an entire race of people. Beyond heinous, were the sadistic minds of Hitler's underlings, particularly medical doctors, who, under the guise of biological research, subjected so many innocent victims—including children—to the most inhumane and diabolical experiments and surgeries. In 1942, Nazi physician Dr. Sigmund Rascher wanted to determine the absolute human tolerance for cold temperature. His purpose was to determine how long Luftwaffe pilots could survive when downed into a cold sea. Jewish prisoners, as well as other internees, were submerged in vats of ice for two to five hours until they lost muscle control and consciousness. Their body temperatures were monitored throughout. Similar tests were performed in air tight cambers to observe the body's reaction to high and low pressure. At extremely low pressure, the victims would tear out their hair, scratch their faces with their nails, beat their heads against the wall until unconscious Upon raising the pressure, the subjects would hemorrhage. Their deaths were agonizing. It leaves one aghast to even imagine such repugnant disregard for human beings who were used as guinea pigs in even more evil exercises. I choose not to mention other experiments performed on reproductive organs—too horrifying to describe. This afront to, and disregard of human dignity is repulsive and beyond the imagination of sane people. In another heinous practice, cuts were made deliberately into the skin of prisoners to create an open wound into which were rubbed broken glass, sawdust, and bits of fabric. The purpose was to measure the rate of infection. In other instances, tuberculosis bacilli were applied to the armpit, as well as inserted directly and forcibly into the throat and lungs by a tube. The same was performed to create infections of malaria, typhoid fever, cholera, diphtheria viral hepatitis. The most diabolical of all experimenters was Dr. Mengele who chose twins and dwarfs on whom to perform surgeries also too shocking for me to describe. I will only say, that one of each set of twins was left with only one leg on which to hop, hence earning the label "rabbits." Even more despicable was how Mengele first won their trust, even having them call him "father." Regretfully, the list of sadistic Nazi crimes against humanity goes on and on—too numerous and ghastly to catalogue—too ugly to remember, but too dangerous to forget

Acknowledgements

A lthough this is a work of historical fiction, parts are based on real people and actual events. First, the facts given in Chapter 25 are taken from the book: *Suzanne's Children: A Daring Rescue in Nazi Paris* by Anne Nelson (2017). It focuses on the underground work of Belgian Catholic patriot Suzanne Spaak who joined the French Resistance in rescuing the Jewish orphans of those deported to concentration camps and executed. Honored in Israel as one of the Righteous Among Nations for her selfless work, she was executed in prison in Fresnes in August 1944.

I previously mentioned a trip I took to Provence in 2014, where I toured a village in the French countryside. A local guide brought us to the home of her grandmother, atop a hill with a narrow road leading down to a café/bar which was requisitioned as the headquarters for the Gestapo during the German occupation of that village. This house was the model for Grand-mere's home on the Rue Savoir in my story. That home and street still exist today (although not by that name) and indeed the house was a haven for Jewish escapees who were hidden between the walls. Moreover, in this same town, was the square where the teenage boys, like my character Jacques, were executed for their subterfuge and pranks against the German occupiers. It was sobering to see the bullet holes still gaping from the stone walls of the open enclosure where they were lined up to be shot.

Most significant was my friendship with Rosa Cotton, now 90 years old, who as a young girl of 14, served as a messenger for the underground against the Nazis. I have dedicated this book to her since I have relied on her recollections for many details in my story.

The years about which I have written were indeed perilous times replete with victimization, prejudice, brutality, savagery, and inhumanity on a gargantuan scale. I have heard time and again the sentiment expressed—"Enough. Enough"—regarding the rehashing, dissection, assignment of blame, and causes for the Holocaust. But I answer, "NEVER, NEVER ENOUGH." As people like Rosa and those of her generation pass away, there is more need than ever to remind those who are born long after that horrendous period of what transpired in those years. Suzanne Spaak was one courageous and selfless individual who, due to her wealth, social position, and non-Jewish background, could easily have ignored the plight of the persecuted and hunted; however, she chose to combat evil with her personal support, her money, and indeed her very life to rescue those in desperate need of her aid. May she rest in peace.

Note: The location of many of the significant events in my story is Grand-mere's house at the top of Rue Savoir, a street name I deliberately chose for its connotative meaning. In French *savoir* means "knowing or to know." From their perch at the top of the hill, my characters—Grand-mere, Jeanne Marie, and her brother Jacques—saw and **knew** all that was going on at the German headquarters below. Of more significance, they used their home as a haven to **save/rescue** those in need. In this way, I felt my selection for the name of their street most apt and suitable in both a literary and metaphoric sense.

ABOUT THE AUTHOR

A teacher of writing and literature for 35 years, Donna DeLeo Bruno has loved books and relished reading for as far back as she can remember. Since retirement, she shares her immense enjoyment and keen appreciation of books and writing styles, with presentations at libraries, book clubs, and women's groups. Donna earned a BA in English from Rhode Island College, an MA equivalency from combined studies at the University of Rhode Island, Providence College, Salve Regina College, and Roger Williams University, as well as a Critic Teacher's Certificate from Brown University (Extension), all in Rhode Island. A poet, essayist, and short story writer, she has been published in Goose River Press Anthology 2015 - 2018. In addition, she is a book reviewer for East Bay Newspapers (Rhode Island) and The John Knox Village Gazette (Florida). She and her husband split their time between Ft. Lauderdale, Florida and their native Bristol, Rhode Island.

Made in the USA
Columbia, SC
29 October 2018